FLOW

GRIP TRILOGY BOOK 1

KENNEDY RYAN

GRIP TRILOGY

Read the Full *Grip* Trilogy!
FREE in Kindle Unlimited!

The Complete Grip Trilogy is available in KU:
All (3) books
US: https://amzn.to/2Gh3Rrs
Worldwide: http://mybook.to/TheGripBoxSet

FLOW (Grip #1)
GRIP (Grip #2)
STILL (Grip #3)

*Audiobooks available for all 3 titles.
Check Audible Escape to listen FREE with subscription!

ALSO BY KENNEDY RYAN

The SOUL Trilogy

Want Rhyson's story? Two musicians chasing their dreams and catching each other?

Dive into the Soul Trilogy!

(Rhyson + Kai)

(FREE in Kindle Unlimited)

My Soul to Keep (Soul 1)*

Down to My Soul (Soul 2)*

Refrain (Soul 3)

Available in Audible Escape!

ALL THE KING'S MEN WORLD

Love stories spanning decades, political intrigue, obsessive passion. If you loved the TV show *SCANDAL*, this series is for you!

The Kingmaker (Duet Book 1: Lennix + Maxim)

FREE in KU!

Ebook, Audio & Paperback

mybook.to/TheKingmakerKindle

The Rebel King (Duet Book 2: Lennix + Maxim)

FREE in KU!

Ebook, Audio & Paperback

mybook.to/RebelKingKindle

Queen Move (Standalone Couple: Kimba + Ezra)

https://geni.us/QueenMovePlatforms

The Killer & The Queen

(Standalone Novella - Grim + Noelani)

Coming Soon!

(co-written with Sierra Simone)

www.subscribepage.com/TKandTQ

HOOPS Series

(Interconnected Standalone Stories set in the explosive world of professional basketball!)

LONG SHOT (A HOOPS Novel)

Iris + August's Story

Ebook, Audio & Paperback:

https://kennedyryanwrites.com/long-shot/

BLOCK SHOT (A HOOPS Novel)

Banner + Jared's Story

Ebook, Audio & Paperback

http://kennedyryanwrites.com/block-shot/

HOOK SHOT (A HOOPS Novel)

Lotus + Kenan's Story

Ebook, Audio & Paperback

http://kennedyryanwrites.com/hook-shot/

HOOPS Holiday (A HOOPS Novella)

Avery + Decker's Story

http://kennedyryanwrites.com/hoops-holiday/

Order Signed Paperbacks

THE BENNETT SERIES

When You Are Mine (Bennett 1)

Loving You Always (Bennett 2)

Be Mine Forever (Bennett 3)

Until I'm Yours (Bennett 4)

COPYRIGHT

Cover Art:
Najla Qamber
Qamber Designs

Cover Photos:

Sarah Zimmerman Photo

Editing:
Angela Smith, Word Whisperer

Proofreading/Copyediting:
Ashley Williams, AW Editing
Paige Maroney Smith

Never miss sales, new releases,
and get a free book every month!

Join Kennedy's mailing list.

AUTHOR'S NOTE

MY JOURNEY AS a writer began with poetry. I remember stumbling across a stack of poems my father had written in college. He's a brilliant man with a couple of master's degrees and a doctorate. I've always known he was intelligent with a sharp mind, obviously, but the poems revealed his soul. It was a treasure, and provoked me to try my hand at it. Those first poems of mine were pretty sad. I've gotten a little better. There are two original pieces that I wrote or co-wrote in GRIP, but the poem I want you to pay special attention to in FLOW is by Pablo Neruda, one of my all-time favorites. Because of copyright protections, I could not include the actual lines from his poem, but I have hyperlinked the title and hope you will take a few moments to read it in full. Poetry is still like magic to me, and I hope you enjoy the greats who inspired me as I was writing.

1

GRIP

IT'S JUST ONE of those days.

Monica's singing in my head. I'm relying on nineties R&B to artic-ulate myself. I'm that hungry. My mouth waters when I think of the huge burrito I was this close to shoveling down my throat before I got the call. My stomach adds a rumble sound effect to the hunger.

I visually pick through the dense LAX crowd, carefully checking each baggage claim carousel. No sign of her. Or at least what I think she might look like.

Rhyson still hasn't texted me his sister's picture. If I know my best friend—and I do—he probably doesn't have a picture of her on his phone. He wouldn't want to admit that, knowing how important family is to me, so I bet he's scrambling to find one. They are the weirdest family I've ever met, which is saying something since mine is no Norman Rockwell painting. I've never actually met any of the Gray family except Rhys and his Uncle Grady. Rhyson's parents and sister still live in New York, and he hasn't seen them in years. Not since he emancipated. We don't "emancipate" where I come from. Nah. We keep shit simple and just never come home. Worked for my dad. He didn't even wait till I was born to leave. Less messy and fewer legal fees. But we didn't have a fortune to fight over like the Grays did.

My phone rings, and I answer, still scanning the crowd for a girl fitting Rhyson's vague description.

"Whassup, Rhys." I clutch the phone and crane my neck to see over what must be a college basketball team. Not one of them is under six five. Even at six two, I can't see the forest for the trees with trees this tall.

"Trying to finish this track. Bristol there yet?" That note in Rhyson's voice tells me this conversation only holds half his attention. He's in the studio, and when he's there, good luck getting him to think about anything other than music. I get it. I'm the same way.

"I don't know if she's here or not. Did you forget to send the picture?"

"Oh, yeah. The picture." He clears his throat to make way for whatever excuse he's about to give me. "I thought I had it on my phone. Maybe I accidentally deleted it or something."

Or something. I let him get away with that. Rhyson's excuse for sending me to pick his sister up from the airport is legit. There's this pop star diva who needs a shit ton of tracks remastered at the last minute before her album drops, but I suspect he's also nervous about his sister's visit. Maybe this emergency is a convenient way to avoid dealing with her for a little bit. Or inconvenient, if you were me and missed lunch rushing to get to the airport as stand-in chauffeur.

"Well, I don't know what she looks like." I push my sunglasses onto the top of my head.

"She looks like me," he says. "I told you we're twins. Lemme check the Cloud for a picture."

Did dude just seriously say 'check the Cloud'?

"Yeah, Rhys, you check the Cloud. Lemme know what you find."

"Okay," he says from the other end, and I can tell he's back into that track. "I called to tell her you were coming, but I keep getting voice mail. I'll try again and send a pic."

Once he hangs up, I concentrate on searching methodically through the crowd. She'd be coming from New York, so I've narrowed it down to one carousel. "She looks like me" isn't much to go on, but I stop at every tall, dark-haired girl, and check for signs of Rhyson's DNA. Hell, she could be right in front of—

That thought fizzles out when my eyes land on the girl standing right in front of me.

Shit.

Black skinny jeans cling to long, lean legs that start at Monday and stretch all the way through next week. A white T-shirt peeps through the small opening left by the black leather jacket molding her arms and chest.

And the rack.

The leather lovingly cups the just-right handful of her breasts. Narrow waist and nice ass. She's not as thick as the chicks I usually pull, but my eyes involuntarily scroll back up her slim curves, seeking the face that goes with this body.

Fuck. This woman is profanely gorgeous.

I never understood the big deal with high cheekbones. I mean, they're cheekbones, not tits. You can't motorboat cheekbones, but now I get it. Her face makes me get it. The bones are molded into a slanting curve that saves her face from angularity and elevates it to arresting. Her mouth, a wide, full line, twists to one side as she scans the crowd around her with eyes so light a shade of gray they're almost silver. Dark, copper-streaked hair frames her face and slips past her shoulders.

The alert from my phone interrupts my ogling. It's a text from Rhyson.

RHYSON: Here ya go. This pic's old as hell, but she can't look much different.

WHEN THE PHOTO COMES OVER, it confirms in my nearly agnostic mind what my mother has been trying to tell me for years. There must indeed be a God. How did I ever doubt Him? He has sent me, little old me, a tiny miracle to confirm His existence. It isn't water into wine, but I'll take it. I toss my eyes up to the sky and whisper a quick thanks to the Big Guy. Because the girl in the family picture, though almost a decade younger and with braces and frizzier hair, is the gorgeous, willowy woman standing in front of me in baggage claims. One hand on her hip and a frown between her dark eyebrows, she leans to peer down the conveyor that now holds only a few bags.

"Dammit," she mutters, pulling her hair off her neck and twisting it into a knot on her head. "I don't need this today."

"We were on the same flight," a guy offers from beside her, his eyes crawling up and down her body in a way that even makes me feel violated. "My luggage still hasn't come either. Maybe we could—"

"Don't." The look she gives him should wither his hard-on. "It's so not happening."

"I was just thinking if you—"

"I know what you were just thinking." She turns away from him to search the conveyor belt again. "You've been just thinking it since we left New York, and not hiding it. So again, I'll say ..."

She turns back to him with a look that would singe the fuzz off your balls.

"Don't."

I like her already. The guy is sputtering and still trying, but he has no game. It's sad really. Guys who have no game.

"Bristol," I say her name with confidence because I can already tell that's the only thing she'll respond to.

Her head jerks around, and those silvery eyes give me a thorough up and down sliding glance. After she's made it all the way down to my classic Jordans and back to my face, she looks just behind and beyond me, as if she isn't sure she actually heard her name or that I'm the one who said it.

"Bristol," I say again, stepping a little closer. "I'm Grip, a friend of your brother's. Rhyson sent me."

Her eyes widen then narrow, the frown deepening.

"Is he okay?" she demands. "Did something happen?"

"No, he's just tied up." I smile to reassure her, hoping she'll smile in return. I want to see her smile. To see how those braces worked out for her.

"Tied up?" Those full lips tighten, still showing me no teeth. She shakes her head a little, huffing a quick breath and stepping closer to the conveyor. "Figures. So you're stuck with me, huh? Sorry."

"I'm not." At least not now that I've seen her. I wouldn't have missed this for my burrito.

She gives me the same knowing look she leveled on No-Game guy. Like guys have been looking at her like that for a long time. Like she can smell lust from fifty paces. Like she's telling me it isn't happening.

Oh, it's happening, baby girl.

I'm plotting all the ways I'll convince her to go out with me, and then who knows where that'll lead when I remember. This is Rhyson's sister. Shit. The hottest girl I've met in ages, and I should probably try not to sleep with her.

Okay. I'm agnostic again. Sorry, Ma.

"I'm waiting for my luggage." She runs a hand over the back of her neck the way I've seen Rhyson do a million times when he's agitated. I note all the other things about her that remind me of my best friend. Let's just say Rhyson's DNA looks a helluva lot better on her. I mean, he's a good-looking guy, but he's, well, a guy. If I rolled that way, maybe. But I roll her way, and dayyyyyum.

"Here's mine," No-Game pipes up with a smug smile when he pulls his big square suitcase from the line.

Bristol creases a fake smile at him that disintegrates as soon as she looks back to the belt.

"Mine shouldn't be far behind then," she says.

"Unless it's lost," No-Game sneers but can't seem to drag his beady eyes from her rack.

"You got your luggage," I say, looking down at him. "How 'bout you step off?"

His blue eyes hiding behind the round glasses do a quick survey of me. I know what he sees and probably what he thinks. Big black dude, arms splashed with tats, "First Weed. Then Coffee" T-shirt. He's probably ready to piss himself. He's like the Diary of a Wimpy Kid all grown up but still wimpy. I could squash him with my eyelashes. It seems we've arrived at the same conclusion because No-Game Wimpy Diary guy turns without a word and pulls his suitcase behind him, docile as a lamb.

"Impressive." Bristol smirks but still doesn't flash teeth. "Been trying to shake that jerk since La Guardia. I felt like spritzing every time he looked at me."

"Spritzing?"

She makes a spraying motion toward her face.

"Yeah, like to refresh your ... never mind." She rolls her eyes and sighs. "Anyway, he may look harmless, but I bet under all that geek he is a nasty piece of work. Unfortunately, it only takes money, not actual class, to fly first class."

I've never flown first class, so I wouldn't know. Come to think of it, I've only flown once. Ma sent me to Chicago to visit her cousins the summer my cousin Chaz died. That was a bad summer. I don't know if it was the heat, but The Crips and The Bloods made our hood a jungle that year. They may have been hunting each other, but a lot of innocent blood ran down our streets. Not that they cared. Not that they ever cared. Ma took all the money she'd been saving from braiding hair to get me out of Compton that summer, and I think I flew Ghetto Air. Whatever shitty aircraft that little bit of extra money got me on, that's what I flew. Not that Chi-Town was less violent, but at least it didn't hold any memories for me. You don't dream other people's nightmares. And in my own bed, I'd wake up every night hearing the shot that killed Chaz just outside my window.

"Finally." Bristol's voice brings me back. "Here it is."

An Eiffel-tower sized Louis Vuitton suitcase ambles down the conveyor belt.

"I thought you were just here for a week?" I lift one brow in her direction.

"I am."

"You sure? 'Cause I could fit my whole apartment in that big-ass suitcase coming at us like a meteor."

"Very funny." A teasing grin pulls at the corners of her bright eyes. "Maybe that says more about your apartment than it does about my suitcase."

The one-room hovel I call home right now appears in my mental window.

"You might be right about that," I admit with a laugh, grabbing the colossal suitcase when it reaches us and setting it on the floor. "Shit. You pack your whole sorority in here?"

"I'm not in a sorority, but thanks for the stereotype." She reaches for the handle, and her hand rests on top of mine. Both our eyes drop to where her slim fingers contrast with my rougher, larger ones.

You know that electric tingle people talk about? That thing that zips up your spine like a tiny shock when your hands first touch? That isn't this touch. It isn't electric. It's something that ... simmers. A heat that kind of seethes under my skin for a second and then explodes into a solar flare. I watch her face to see if she's feeling anything. If she does, she hides it well. If she's anything like her brother, hiding things is a habit. Her expression doesn't change when she tugs the handle until her hand slips from under mine.

"It's got wheels." She pulls the suitcase toward her and finally meets my eyes. "My feminist sensibilities tell me to carry it myself."

"Maybe my manhood won't let me walk idly by while a delicate lady carries her own suitcase." I shrug. "I got a rep to protect."

"Oh, I don't doubt you have a rep." Bristol's brows arch high and her lips twist into a smirk. "Where to?"

I grab the suitcase by the handle, pulling it from her grasp, and start walking. When I look over my shoulder, her narrowed eyes rest on the mammoth suitcase I've commandeered. The defiant light in her eye makes me want to commandeer her like I just did this over-priced baggage. This is Rhyson's sister. I need to keep reminding myself she should be squarely placed in the NO FUCK bin. But, damn, if all bets were off, she'd be feeling me every time she walked for a week.

If things were different. But they're not.

So I won't.

I'm just gonna keep telling myself that.

2

BRISTOL

I'M MORE THAN capable of dragging my luggage around, but I appreciate the view as I watch Grip do it for me. My eyes inevitably stray to the tight curve of his ass in the sweatpants dripping from his hips. His back widens from a taut waist, the muscles flexing beneath the outrageous T-shirt hugging his torso and stretching at the cut of his bicep.

Ever since he called my name and I looked up into eyes the color of darkened caramel, I haven't drawn nearly enough air. Soot-black eyebrows and lashes so long and thick they tangle at the edges frame those eyes. Lips, sculpted and full. Some concoction of cocoa and honey swirl to form the skin stretched tightly over the strong bones of his face. I'm almost distracted enough by all this masculine beauty to not be pissed at my twin brother.

Almost.

Five years. I haven't seen Rhyson outside of a courtroom in five years, haven't even spoken to him since Christmas. I finally initiate this visit to him in Los Angeles, and he sends some stranger for me? I fall into step beside Grip so I can read his expression when I drill him. In profile, he's almost even better, a tantalizing geometry of angles and slopes. He tosses a quick look to me from the side, a caramel-drenched gaze that melts down the length of my body before returning to my face, stealing more air from my lungs.

"So, why couldn't Rhyson come get me?" I ask.

"Long story short," Grip says as we reach the exit. "The album Rhyson's been working on—"

"He's working on an album?" A grin takes over my face. "I didn't know he was working on new music. Piano, I assume? I can't wait to hear—"

"It's for someone else," Grip corrects. "He's producing an album for an artist, and her label wants all these changes before it drops. Some remastering, maybe some other stuff."

"Oh, I was hoping he was back to performing. Doing his own music." I narrow my eyes and nod decisively. "He should be."

I'm actually here in part to convince him of it. I'm staking my entire college degree and career aspirations on him seeing things my way. People usually do see things my way if I play my cards right. My mother taught me to play my cards right. She may not be much of a mother, but she's a helluva card shark.

"He will one day." Grip offers me a small smile. "When he's ready."

"You think so?" I hope so. "Yeah."

He drags my suitcase toward an ancient Jeep with a mountain-sized airport security guard standing in front of it.

"Thanks, man." Grip pounds fists and accepts keys from the guy. He glances up and down the busy sidewalk. "Anybody give you shit yet about the car being here?"

"Nah." The guard gives a quick head shake. "You know I run this place."

"Yeah right." Grip sketches a quick grin. "Well, thanks."

"No problem, bruh." The guard's eyes flick to and over me briefly before returning to Grip, brows lifted in a silent query.

"Oh, Amir, this is Bristol, Rhyson's sister." Grip waves a hand between us. "Bristol, Amir. We grew up together. He made sure my car wasn't towed while I came to get you. It was all kind of last minute."

At the last minute, Rhyson decided he would delegate me to strangers. I swallow my disappointment and spit out a smile.

"Nice to meet you, Amir." I extend my hand, and he brings it to his lips in unexpected gallantry.

"The pleasure is all mine." Amir grins roguishly, his eyes teasing from beneath a fall of dreadlocks. "You didn't tell me Rhyson's sister looked like this."

"Didn't know." Grip laughs and hauls my huge suitcase into the back of the Jeep. "The operative words being 'Rhyson's sister', so pick your jaw up and say 'Goodbye, Bristol.'"

"Goodbye, Bristol." A delightful smile creases Amir's face. "Goodbye, Amir." I can't help but reciprocate with a wide grin of

my own. Amir salutes and makes his way back inside the airport. When I glance back to Grip, he's leaning against the dilapidated Jeep watching me closely, traces of a smile lingering on his handsome face.

"What?" I quirk an eyebrow as the smile melts from my face. "Nothing." His shoulders push up and drop, languid and powerful. "Just thinking those braces worked out well for you."

"Braces?" My fingers press against my lips. "How'd you know I used to wear braces?"

Grip hands me his phone, and if I didn't have enough reasons to string Rhyson up, sending "ugly stage" adolescence pictures to his hot friend gives me another. Once I get past embarrassment for my twelve-year-old, frizzy-haired, flat-chested self, I really study the picture more closely. It's a rare family photo, and I remember the day we took it with absolute clarity. Rhyson was home off the road for a few weeks. We'd known since he was three years old what an extraordinarily talented pianist he would be, but it was only around eleven that he actually started touring all over the world. Music is a family business for us, and my parents went with him on the road as his managers. I, however, had no talent to speak of, so I stayed home with a nanny who made sure I ate, went to school, and had a "normal" childhood. As normal as your childhood can be when your parents barely remember you exist.

"Rhys sent that so I could identify you at the airport." Grip holds out his hand for his phone.

I study the photo another few seconds. Rhyson looks like he'd rather be anywhere but with the three of us. Just a few years after that picture was taken, he would find a way to leave us. To leave me. As much as I told myself over and over that he emancipated from our parents, not from me, that never made me feel less abandoned or less alone in our sprawling New York home. After he moved to California to live with my father's twin brother, Grady, I'd sit in the music room at his piano, straining my ears for the memory of him rehearsing in there for hours every day. Eventually, I stopped going in that room. I draped his piano in white cloth, locked the door, and stopped chasing his music. Stopped chasing him. I told myself that if he wanted to be my brother again, he'd call. Except he never did, so I called him. It hurts to feel so connected to someone who obviously doesn't feel as connected to me.

"You okay, Bristol?"

Grip's question tugs my mind free of that tumultuous time in my family that felt like a civil war. His hand is still extended, waiting.

"Sorry, yeah." I drop the phone into his palm, careful to avoid actual skin-to-skin contact. Based on how my body responded to the brush of his fingers when he took my suitcase, I suspect he could easily fry me with another touch. "Just feeling sorry for that geeky little girl in the picture."

"Oh, don't cry for her," he says with a grin. "I have it on good authority when she grows up the braces are gone and she has a beautiful smile."

I roll my eyes so he won't think his lines are actually working on me, though he does actually make me feel a little better.

He opens the passenger door and I slide in, catching a whiff of him as I go. It's fresh and clean and man. No cologne that I can detect. All Grip.

"So where to now?" He starts the old Jeep but lets it idle while he turns radio knobs, searching for a station.

"Food." I blow out a weary breath as the long trip and lack of food hit me hard. "I hope Grady's got food at his house."

Grip's eyes widen just a bit before sliding away from me.

"Uh, there may not be a ton of food at Grady's place." Grip taps his long fingers on the steering wheel. "He's kind of out of town."

"Out of town?" I snap my head around to stare at his rugged profile. "He knew I was coming, right? How can he be . . .what?"

My father and his twin brother, Grady, weren't close before, but after Rhyson emancipated from my parents to live with him, our relationship with him grew even more strained. My parents resented him "taking" Rhyson away, and I haven't seen him either. I never had much of a relationship with my uncle, and it doesn't look like that will change on this particular trip.

"A colleague had a death in the family," Grip says. "He needed Grady to step in for him at a songwriters' conference."

A piece of lead rests heavily on my chest, constricting my breath for a second. Why am I even here? It's obvious I'm the only one looking for any connection, any reconciliation for our family.

"He couldn't have anticipated this," Grips adds hastily.

"I get it." I force a stiff curve to my lips and stare out the passenger side window so Grip doesn't see the smile never reaches my eyes. "This is gonna be some family reunion. Uncle Grady away and Rhyson ... tied up."

"We don't cry in front of strangers."

My mother's voice echoes back to me from childhood. We don't cry in front of anyone, truth be told. I blink furiously and sniff discreetly, hoping a red nose isn't betraying the stupid emotion swelling in my belly and pushing up into my chest. I must be PMSing. I suckled at my mother's iron tit. Something this insubstantial after all I've been through shouldn't affect me this way. I know not to wear my emotions in places people can see them. And yet, here I am, against my mother's wishes and advice, clear across the country, risking parts of my heart with family who apparently don't give a damn about me.

"Bristol, Grady will be back soon and Rhyson will be around." I hate the deliberate gentleness of Grip's tone. It's as if he sees my cracks and knows that at any minute I might break.

Red nose and teary eyes or not, I'll show him I won't break. I'll make sure he knows I'm stronger that that. That I don't need my brother or my uncle. That they are the ones who missed out on knowing me.

I whip around to tell him so, to unload my defenses and assurances on him, but all my bravado slams into the compassion of his eyes. More disconcerting than how beautiful his eyes are, is how much they seem to see. How much they seem to know. The bitter words die on my tongue. I swallow the shattered syllables. I swallow the pain. With practice, it goes down easy, lubricated by tears I'll never shed. I've had lots of practice. I've had lots of tears, but this stranger, this beautiful stranger, won't see. I steady my trembling mouth and level my eyes until they meet his stare squarely.

"I'm hungry. Are we going to eat, or what?"

I know I sound like the spoiled sorority girl he assumed I was, but whatever. Talking about food is highly preferable to discussing my family drama, which goes back too far and down too deep. Especially on an empty stomach.

He shifts his glance back to the line of cars pulling away from the airport. Those full lips don't tug into the easy smile he showed me before. I regret making things heavy. Shit got too real, too fast.

"Sure." Eyes ahead, he shifts from park to drive and pulls away from the curb. "I know just the place. Food's great."

Maybe to distract myself from the familiar disappointment sitting alongside the hunger in my belly, I run my eyes discreetly over all six feet and however many inches of him. He's nothing like the guys I've dated, but gorgeous nonetheless. He tucks his bottom lip between an even row of white teeth, concentrating on the ever-hellish LA traffic. As much as I know I shouldn't, I imagine biting that bottom lip.

Am I hungry? Oh, yeah.

3

BRISTOL

ALL THOSE CAUTIONARY tales about stranger danger apparently didn't take because I'm currently cruising down the I-5 with a man I met only minutes ago, who may have the face and body of a lower level deity but has not provided any real proof that he actually knows my brother. Yet, how else would he have known my name? And he did have that hideous throwback picture on his phone. I'm fairly certain he's no Ted Bundy, but I could have at least asked to speak with Rhyson to confirm. I slide a surreptitious glance his way, studying the hands on the steering wheel. Those hands are grace and capability, rough and smooth. Doesn't mean they wouldn't wring my neck ...

"So, how did you say you know my brother again?" I ask, deliberately nonchalant.

"I was wondering when you'd get around to asking some questions." His expression loosens into a grin. "You keep looking at me like I might pull over at the next rest stop and stuff you in the trunk."

"Who ... what ... me? Noooo."

He breaks away from the traffic long enough to give me a knowing look, accompanied by a smirk.

"Okay, maybe a little." A nervous laugh slips out. "I actually was thinking I should have asked for some proof or ID or something. Not just hopped in the car with a perfect stranger."

"Perfect?" Cockiness curves his lips. "I get that a lot." "You're so full of yourself, aren't you?" I laugh.

"Oh, I shouldn't be?" Even in profile, his grin is a little dazzling. "No, you're right. I could have offered more than 'I'm Grip. Let's eat.'"

He tips his head toward the phone in my lap.

"Why don't you call Rhys so you can breathe a little easier?"

I should have thought of that. What's wrong with me? Maybe subconsciously there's some part of me that's hesitant to call, dreading those first awkward moments when Rhyson and I have no idea what to say to each other. When it becomes terribly apparent I no longer know my twin brother and he no longer knows me.

If he ever really did.

"It's ringing," I tell Grip, phone pressed to my ear.

"Bristol?" My brother's deep voice rumbles from the other end. Even arranging this trip we talked very little, coordinating most of it by email and text. Hearing his voice, knowing I'll see him, affects me more deeply than I thought it would. He has no idea how much I've missed him. Emotion blisters my throat. Even though we haven't talked much the last few years, he sounds the way he always did when I would slip into his rehearsal room while he was playing. Exhausted and distracted.

"Yeah. It's me." I draw a deep breath and dive in. "So, you couldn't break away long enough to meet your long-lost sister at the airport, huh?"

"Lost sister?" Rhyson emits a disbelieving puff of air. "You? Lost? Never."

He really has no idea. No one does.

"I would have been there," Rhyson continues. "I made sure I'd be done with this by the time you landed, but this artist and her label are riding me hard about remastering—"

"Yeah, I heard," I cut in. "It's fine. I'll see you when you're done. You will be done soon, right?"

"Uh ... soon? Sure. Relatively soon."

That could mean anything from tonight to next year when Rhyson's immersed in music. At least, that used to be the case, but I doubt much has changed.

"Then I guess I'll see you when I see you." I try to keep the disappointment and irritation out of my voice, but Rhyson's sigh on the other end lets me know I fail.

"Bristol, I'm sorry. I'll see you at Grady's tonight, okay? And I promise we'll catch up tomorrow."

"So you'll be done tomorrow?" My heart lifts the tiniest bit. I don't want to sound needy, but he's the whole reason I'm here. Against my parents' advice, against my better judgment, I'm seeking him out. I've crossed the damn country to try. If I don't try, who will in what's left of our family?

"Not sure if everything will be wrapped today or not," he says. "I'll send them the tracks, but they may have more tweaks. We'll see."

"Sure." I clip the word. "We'll see."

"In the meantime, you're okay?" Rhyson sounds half in the conversation, like the music is already siren calling him.

I flick a glance Grip's way. His expression is completely relaxed and impassive, and his eyes are set on the road like I'm not even there, but he doesn't fool me. There's this constant alertness that crackles around him, as if he's been trained to be on guard but is wily enough to let you believe he isn't. I think he's always completely aware of everything around him, and this conversation between Rhyson and me is no exception.

"Yeah, we're on our way to eat." I fiddle with the strap on my bag. "Since apparently Grady isn't home either."

"Yeah." Guilt drags Rhyson's one-word reply out. "That was completely unexpected. He—"

"Grip explained," I insert before he rehashes the story I've already heard. "The conference. I know. Things happen. Well, I guess I'll see you at Grady's place ...your place ...tonight," I finally say.

"Great. Can I speak to Marlon?"

"Marlon?" I frown, wondering if I really should have been more cautious before getting in the car. "Um ... someone named Grip picked me up."

Rhyson chuckles, and I notice Grip's mouth hitch to the side, even though he doesn't turn his head.

"Marlon is his real name. You think his mom named him Grip?"

"How would I know what his mom named him?" I laugh and meet Grip's eyes briefly, finding them smiling back at me.

"Here ya go." I proffer my phone. "For you, Marlon."

He stops my heart for a beat with a stretch of white teeth and full lips.

Wow. That's just not fair.

"'Sup, Rhys." He nods, his smile melting a little every few seconds and a small pull of his brows making me wonder what Rhyson's saying. "All right. Yeah. We'll grab something to eat. I got you."

He offers one more grunt and a mumbled "peace" before handing the phone back to me.

"Hey," I say once I have the phone back.

"Yeah. Hey," Rhyson says. "I actually did have dinner planned for us. You still like Mexican?"

"I love Mexican." I'm pleasantly surprised that he remembers.

"Well, maybe we'll get to try this place before you go back, but with the emergency on this project . . ." He sighs heavily. "Anyway, Marlon will take you to eat and then bring you to Grady's and stay with you till I get home."

"He doesn't need to do that." I hate feeling like a burden to anyone, and right now, I feel like the egg baby project Grip has to keep alive. "I'll be fine on my own."

"Marlon doesn't mind," Rhyson assures me. "He has stuff to do for Grady anyway. He helps with one of his music classes."

I just bet he does. Lies. I glance at Grip's profile, a study in impassivity.

"Gotta go," Rhyson says. "See you later if you're still awake when I get home. I'm sure you're exhausted."

"Yeah. More hungry than anything."

"Marlon will take care of you." A voice in the background interrupts Rhyson. "Hey, I need to go. See you tonight."

"Okay. Tonight." I hold the phone to my ear for a few seconds after he's gone just because I don't want to talk.

I finally drop the phone to my lap, processing the longest conversation I've had with my twin brother in five years. I have no idea what's going through Grip's mind. It's too quiet, so I break the silence with the lightest question I can think of.

"Marlon, huh?" I ask with a smile.

"Only Rhyson calls me by my real name." He keeps his eyes ahead on the road, grimacing good-naturedly. "And my mom."

"And Grip, where'd that come from?"

"I was in a talent show or showcase or some shit when I was a kid." He laughs, shaking his head at the memory. "I had to recite a poem and was so nervous, I kept holding onto the mic even after I was done. Just wouldn't let go. Maybe it was like my safety blanket. Who knows? One of the kids started calling me 'Grip' after the show, and it stuck."

"So even then you were craving the spotlight," I tease.

"I guess so." His smile fades after a few seconds. He looks briefly away from the road and at me. "I don't mind, ya know. Staying, I mean. There's things I can do in the rehearsal room at Grady's house."

I don't bother arguing, because I seriously doubt I'll change his mind now that Rhyson has asked him. I just nod and pretend to check the email on my phone.

"We're here." Grip pulls into a parking space and cuts the engine.

I look up from my phone, surprised to see the length of pier stretching from the shore out over the Pacific Ocean.

"Where's here?"

"Mick's. Jimmy, one of our good friends, works here. Food's good."

"Well, that's all I care about."

As we're walking up the boardwalk toward a sign that reads "Mick's" I feel overdressed. In my sleek leather jacket and ankle boots, both black, I'm so very New York. Everyone's milling around in bikinis, tank tops, board shorts, and flip-flops. Once we're seated at a window booth with an ocean view, I slip the jacket off. I sense more than see Grip's eyes linger on my arms and shoulders bared by the sleeveless shirt under my jacket. I force myself to keep my arms at my side and not cross them over my chest. I block his line of vision with the huge menu and feel as if I can breathe a little easier with it between the heat of his eyes and my skin.

"So what's good?" I ask.

"I get the same thing every time. Burger and fries."

I scrunch my nose, not seeing anything I want, but half-starved enough to settle. Before I can say as much, a set of perky breasts in a green bikini appear beside our table. My eyes do the slow crawl from the girl's hot pink toenails in her wedge heels, over the skimpy cut-off denim shorts and the bikini top, which barely bridles her breasts. Bright blue eyes and blonde hair complete the California package. If all the girls look like this, and a quick glance around Mick's dining room tells me a lot of them do, I may reconsider my secret plan to move here when I graduate.

"Hey, dude." Perky tits leans over to drop a quick kiss on Grip's jaw.

"Jim, what's good, girl?" He slaps her ass, aiming a playful smile up at her. "Been missing you."

Rewind. Jimmy's a girl? Her name tag reads "Jimmi." The "i" would be cuter if I wasn't so hungry.

"I know." Jimmi blows at the blonde bangs brushing her eyebrows. "Between shifts here and gigging all over town, there's been no time to hang."

"Yeah, Rhys and I were just saying the same thing," Grip says. "We need to get everybody together."

"My uncle's beach house!" The blue eyes light up. "He's out of the country and said I could crash there some."

"We need to do that for real."

"We could play Scrabble again," she says. "Remember how much fun we had?"

"You sure you want to play Scrabble?" Grip lifts a skeptical brow. "Why wouldn't I?" She looks confused, or maybe that's always her

look. She's very blonde, even if it may be from a bottle, so I can't tell. "You're not really good at it," he says with a grin.

"Why would you say that?" Jimmi's hands go to her hips.

"'Cause you thought 'guffaw' was a character from *Lord of the Rings*."

"Ugh," Jimmi half-groans, half-laughs. "You weren't supposed to tell anybody that."

Oh, my God, guffaw.

Laughter bubbles up in my throat. I try to push it down, but it's no use. It springs from my mouth as a, well . . . guffaw. Jimmi looks a little embarrassed but manages a self-deprecating smile. Grip's laugh matches mine.

"Jim, this is Rhyson's twin sister, Bristol. Bristol, this is Jimmi. She went to high school with Rhys and me."

"Great." Jimmi gives me a wry look. "Now, she'll think I'm an airhead."

I don't deny it and just smile and hold out my hand. "Nice to meet you, Jimmi," I say. "I promise not to tell."

"Well, thanks for that." Jimmi squints an eye and tilts her head, considering me. "Did he say twin sister? I knew Rhyson had a sister, but I had no idea you guys were twins. I see the resemblance."

I'm surprised she's even heard that much about me.

"I live in New York." I attempt a natural smile. "We haven't seen much of each other lately."

Jimmi's smile shrinks, her eyes dropping to the floor.

"Oh, yeah." She nods, avoiding my eyes. "He doesn't get back to New York much, does he?"

"No, not much." I agree quietly since it's obvious she, like everyone else, knows how splintered our family is.

"So where is the maestro?" Jimmi directs the question to Grip. "Last minute remastering with that project he was working on," Grip says.

"Ah." Jimmi nods, a tentative smile on her lips. "I haven't seen him in weeks. I miss him."

"Okay, Jim, you know the deal." Grip's look seems to hold a careful warning.

"I know. I know. You don't have to worry about me." Jimmi waves a dismissive hand in the air and turns back to me. "Did you see anything you want?"

If I'm not mistaken, the anything she wants is my brother, but I just got here, so what do I know? I deliberately shift my eyes to the menu.

"What's good?"

"Let's see." Jimmi leans over my shoulder to consider the menu like she hasn't seen it before. One of her breasts nearly pokes my eye out. I lean back in my seat to avoid a nipple.

"Careful where you aim those things," I say before I catch my wild tongue. I'm great at keeping my thoughts to myself when it counts, but when it doesn't, I don't bother.

Startled blue eyes collide with mine, and I'm not sure if she expects an apology or what, but I just look pointedly from her torpedo tits back up to her face. For a beat, I think I've really offended her, but then she laughs until she has to bend over, giving the customers behind her an eyeful, I'm sure. Grip grins, his eyes affectionate on blonde and breasty.

"Oh, we're gonna be friends." Jimmi wipes the tears at the corner of her eyes. "Watch where I aim ... that's priceless. Okay. You like seafood?"

"Um, yeah." I blink a few times at the speedy shift of gears. "I love it."

"You like scallops?" She drops her voice to a conspiratorial whisper. "Off-menu item."

"I would kill for scallops." My mouth is already watering, and my empty stomach is already thanking her.

"Your server will be over in a sec, but I'll tell her to hook you up." She winks at me before turning back to Grip. "I'm singing in a little bit. They're finally letting me on stage."

She gestures to a small space set up for live music.

"Nice." Grip's smile reflects genuine pleasure. "'Bout time."

"Don't leave before I'm done." She squeezes his shoulder. "I may have a gig for you."

"For real?" He glances down at his beeping phone, a frown wrinkling his forehead before he returns his attention to Jimmi. "My money isn't nearly long enough. I'll do anything but strip."

Jimmi gives him a head tilt and a come-on-now twist of her lips. "Okay, you got me. For the right price, I probably would strip." A devilish smile crinkles his eyes at the corners. "But not my first choice."

"It's deejaying at Brew. Maybe tomorrow night." Jimmi crosses her arms over the menus pressed to her chest. "Could be a regular gig, for a while at least."

"Cool." Grip's glance strays back to his phone, his tone distracted.

"Everything okay?" Jimmi eyes the phone in his hand.

"Yeah." Grip lifts his eyes, splitting a look between the two of us. "Sure. Let's chop it up after your set."

"Okay. How long you here, Bristol?"

"Just a few days. I leave Friday."

"Good!" Jimmi beams. "We'll get to spend some time together."

"I'd like that."

Now that I've gotten past the breasts stuffed into the bikini practically assaulting me, I mean what I say. She seems cool. "Good luck on stage."

We've bonded a little over scallops and tits, so my smile for Jimmi comes more naturally.

"Thanks!" she squeals and wiggles her fingers in a wave. "Gotta go get ready."

"So you and Jimmi went to high school with Rhyson?" I ask, watching Jimmi teeter off on her wedge heels.

"I'm sorry. I thought you knew that." Grip shakes his head. "I really did just kind of grab you and toss you in the car."

"It's fine. I appreciate your help." I peel the paper from the straw Jimmi left on the table, focusing on that instead of looking at

Grip. "I actually know very little about my brother's life since he left."

"What do you want to know?" Grip relaxes, stretching one arm along the back of the booth.

"Lots I guess." I shrug, keeping my voice casual. "I'll let Rhyson tell me his stuff, but what about you? If you were at the School of the Arts, you must be . . .a musician? Dancer? What?"

"I'm Darla, your server," a petite girl says before Grip can respond. "How you guys doing today?"

"Fine, Darla." Grip flashes her a smile, not even trying to be sexy, but Darla melts a little right where she stands. I practically see the puddle. The lashes around her pretty, brown eyes start batting, and I might be too nauseated to eat my scallops.

"I'm fine, too, Darla." I wave a hand since she seems to have forgotten I'm here. "And actually really hungry. Jimmi mentioned scallops. How are they prepared?"

"Scallops?" Darla's brows pinch. "We don't have scallops on the menu."

"No, she said they were an off-menu item." I hold onto my patience even though my stomach is starting to feed on itself as we speak.

"No, we don't—"

"Darla." Grip grabs her hand, stroking his thumb over her palm. "Maybe you could double-check on the scallops because it seemed like Jimmi knew about them."

After Darla visibly shudders, her smile widens and she leans a little toward Grip.

"I am new," she admits shyly. "I could check on it for you."

"I appreciate that." I give her a gentle reminder that they were actually for me, not the man she's salivating over.

Darla's smile slips just a little as she uses the hand Grip isn't holding to retrieve the pad from her back pocket. Obviously reluctant, she drops Grip's hand to pull the pencil from behind her ear.

"And to drink?" She sounds like she'll have to trek to Siberia to fetch whatever I order.

"Water's fine." I look at the tight circle her irritation has made of her mouth. "Bottled, please."

I wouldn't put it past her to spit in it.

"I always get the Mick's Mighty," Grip pipes up. "And fries. Let's just stick with that. And that new craft beer you guys got in."

"A beer?" Darla squints and grins. "Are you twenty-one?"

"I don't know." Grip doesn't look away, seeming to relish how mesmerized our girl Darla is. "Am I?"

Darla eyes him closely. . .or rather even closer, her eyes wandering over the width of shoulders and slipping to crotch level where his legs spread just a little as he leans back. Darla bites her bottom lip before running her tongue across it. This is just sad. Exactly the kind of behavior that could set the women's movement back decades. In Rochester, New York, Susan B. Anthony is turning over in her grave as Darla licks her lip.

"Um, were you still going to check on the scallops?" I give her a pointed look. I mean, seriously. How does she know Grip and I aren't a couple? I'd be insulted if he were mine. Hell, I'm insulted, and he isn't.

Darla shifts hard eyes back to me, heaving a long-suffering sigh and straightening.

"Yeah. I'll go check on the scallops." Her face softens when she looks back to Grip. "And I'll get your order in."

"The beer?" His smile and those eyes wrapped in all that charisma really should be illegal.

"Okay." Darla giggles but still doesn't ask for his ID. "The new craft coming up."

"Well, that was sad for women everywhere," I mumble.

"Don't blame Darla." Grip's cheeky grin foreshadows whatever outrageous thing he's about to say. "Blame all this chocolate charm."

My laugh comes out as a snort. "I'm guessing that's a self-proclaimed moniker."

"I see you're immune to it, but you do catch more bees with honey." Grip offers this sage, if unoriginal, advice. "Or in my case, with chocolate."

"Where'd you read that? *The Player's Guide to Catching Bees*?"

"No, I learned it the way I learn most things." His eyes dim the tiniest bit. "The hard way."

I'm not sure what to say, so I don't say anything for a few seconds, and neither does he. It should be awkward, but it isn't. Our eyes lock in the comfortable silence.

"So before Darla buzzed through," I pause for effect, waiting for his quickly-becoming-familiar grin, "you were telling me about the School of the Arts. You're a musician?"

"I write and rap."

"As in you're a rapper?"

"Wow, they said you were quick," he answers with a grin.

"Oh, sarcasm. My second language." I find myself smiling even though it's been a crappy day with too many complications and not enough food. "So you rap. Like hoes, bitches, and bling?" I joke.

"At least you're open-minded about it," he deadpans.

"Okay. I admit I don't listen to much hip-hop. So convince me there's more to it."

"And it's my responsibility to convince you ... why?" he asks with a grin.

"Don't you want a new fan?" I'm smiling back again. "I just doubt it's your type of music."

"We've known each other all of an hour, and already you're assigning me 'types'. Well, I'm glad you have an open mind about me," I say, echoing his smart-ass comment.

I halfway expect him to volley another reply at me, but he just smiles. I didn't anticipate conversation this stimulating. His body, yes. Conversation, no.

"So are you any good?" I ask. "At rapping, I mean."

"Would you know if I were good?" he counters, a skeptical look on his face.

"Probably not." My laugh comes easier than most things have today. "But I might know if you were bad."

"I'm not bad." He chuckles. "I think my flow's pretty decent." "Sorry," I interject. "For the rap remedial in the audience, define flow."

"Define it?" He looks at me as if I asked him to saddle a unicorn. "Wow. You ever assume you know something so well, that it's so basic, you can't think of how to explain it?"

"Let me guess. That's how it is with flow."

"Well, now that you asked me to define it, yeah."

"Just speak really slowly and use stick figures if you need to." Rich laughter warms his eyes. "Okay. Here goes."

He leans forward, resting those coppery-colored, muscle-corded arms on the table, distracting me. I think I really may need stick figures if he keeps looking this good.

"A rapper's flow is like . . ." He chews his full bottom lip, jiggling it back and forth, as if the action might loosen his thoughts. "It's like the rhythmic current of the song. Think of it as a relationship between the music and the rapper's phrasing or rhythmic vocabulary, so to speak. You make choices about how many phrases you place in a measure. Maybe you want an urgent feeling, so you squeeze a lot of phrasing into a measure. Maybe you want a laid-back feel, and you leave space; you hesitate. Come in later than the listener expects."

"Okay. That makes sense."

"And the choices a rapper makes, how well the current of that music and his phrasing, his rhythmic vocabulary, work together, that's his flow. Cats like Nas, Biggie, Pac—they're in this rarefied category where their flow is so sick, so complex, but it seems easy. That's when you know a flow is exceptional. When it seems effortless."

"Now I get that." I give him a straight face, but teasing eyes. "I can see how you won your rap scholarship."

"Rap scholarship! It sounds so weird when you say it." He sits back in his seat, a smile crooking his lips. "I actually went for writing. Rapping was kind of Rhyson's idea."

"Rhyson?" Shock propels a quick breath out of me. "What does he know about rap?"

"I'm guessing more than you do." His smile lingers for a second before falling away. "I wrote poetry. That's how I got in. Rhyson was looking for a way to translate his classical piano sound to a more modern audience, so I helped him. And he convinced me that all these poems I had could be raps. The rest is history."

"So you have an album or something?"

"Not yet. Working on a mixtape." He clamps a straw between his teeth. "Also working on paying my rent."

"Thus the Deejaying?"

"Deejaying, sweeping floors for studio time, writing for other artists, doing stuff with Grady." A careless shrug of his shoulders. "Whatever comes, I do."

"You write for other artists?" "Yeah."

"I don't get it. Rappers don't write their own stuff? I thought it was so personal and rooted in where you're from and all that."

"To not know much about hip-hop, you have definite ideas about it," he teases.

"You'll find I have definite ideas about everything." I chuckle because it's true. "Even things I know nothing about."

"Ah, so that's a family trait."

He's so right. Rhyson and I are both obstinate know-it-alls. "Apparently." I nod for him to continue. "You were saying."

"So hip-hop's like any other genre. There are some guys who write everything themselves, and it's like what you're describing. But a club's a club's a club. Love is love. Anybody can write it. So sometimes guys like me, who are kind of writers first, we help."

"Would I know any of the songs you've worked on?"

"Probably not." He grins. "Not because they're not on the radio, but because I doubt you listen to those stations."

"You're making a lot of assumptions about someone you just met. Maybe I know all of them. Try me."

He rattles off four songs. I know none of them. Dammit. I'll have to eat crow, which if Darla doesn't get my scallops, I might gladly do.

When Darla returns and confirms that they can provide my scallops, I place my order. The hurried meal I ate this morning is a distant memory, so I dive in as soon as the food arrives, working my way methodically through every morsel on my plate. I eat the scallops so fast you'd think I sprinkled them with fairy dust to make them disappear.

"Remind me to keep you fed." Grip takes another bite of his burger.

"Very funny." I glance up sheepishly from my empty plate. "How's their dessert?"

We share a slow smile, and I can't remember when I've felt this way with another person. Laughing at each other's jokes, comfortable with each other's silences, calling each other out on our crap.

"Grip." A tall man with dark brown skin and eyes to match stops at our table. "I thought that was you."

"What's good, Skeet?" Grip stands, and they grasp hands, exchanging pats to the back. "Haven't seen you in months. Congrats on the new album."

"Man, thanks." Skeet's eyes flick to me. "Who's the little shawty?"

The little shawty? Does he mean me? Grip catches my eye, apparently finding it funny.

"This is Bristol," he answers with a laugh. "Rhyson's sister." "Rhyson, Rhyson. Who's . . ." Skeet frowns for a second before he remembers. "Oh. That white dude who plays the piano?"

Not exactly how I would describe one of the greatest living classical pianists, but we can go with that.

"Yeah, that's him." Grip's smile appreciates the irony of Skeet's description. "Bristol's visiting for the week."

"Nice." Skeet smiles politely before turning his attention back to Grip. "What'd you think of the album?"

Grip screws his face up, a rueful turn to his mouth.

"That bad?" Skeet demands.

"It was a'ight," Grip concedes. "Honestly, I just know you have something better in you than that."

"Well, damn, Grip," Skeet mumbles. "Why don't you tell me what you really think?"

"Oh, okay. Well, that shit was whack," Grip says.

"Um, I was being sarcastic," Skeet says. "But since we being honest. . ."

"We've known each other too long to be anything but honest. It just felt kind of tired." Grip sits and gestures for Skeet to join us. "Who'd you work with?"

"You know that guy Paul?" Skeet sits and steals one of Grip's fries. "They call him Low."

"That dude?" Grip sips his beer and grimaces. "Figures."

"Well, you ain't been around," Skeet says defensively. "I didn't know if you was still down or whatever."

"Am I still down?" Irritation pinches Grip's face into a frown. "I'm the same dude I've always been. I'm working with anybody who can pay, so don't use that as an excuse."

"Right, right, but you know how some of these niggas go off and get all new on you."

My eyes stretch before I have time to disguise my surprise when he uses the N-word so freely in front of me. I squirm in my seat, sip my water, and try to look invisible. That is one of the worst words in the English language, and I would never use it. I've never said it, and I never will. It's hard for me to understand how people of color use it even casually.

"Well, I ain't new." Grip pulls out his phone. "Let's get some dates down to hit the studio. See if we can write some stuff for your next one."

While they set up studio time, I happily consider the dessert menu. I was totally serious. It feels like I haven't eaten in days, and I have room for more.

"Sorry about that," Grips says once Skeet is gone. "But the struggle is real. Don't work, don't eat, so I work whenever the opportunity presents itself."

"Do you really think his album is weak, or did you just say that to drum up business for yourself?"

"Oh, no. The shit's weak as hell." Grip's deep laugh rolls over me and coaxes a smile to my lips. "I don't lie, especially about music. It's the most important thing in my life. It's my gift, so to me it's almost sacred."

"Now I understand how you and Rhyson became so close," I say wryly. "Music always came first with him. Or at least it used to be. I don't pretend to know him anymore. Not that we've ever been that close."

It's quiet for a moment while I pretend to read the dessert menu.

"You love your brother," Grips says softly, drawing my eyes up to his face. "I know guys like us aren't easy to put up with. We lose ourselves in our music. We neglect everything else in our lives, but don't give up on him. Cut him some slack. He's working his ass off."

"I guess I'm not doing a good job of hiding how hard this is, huh?" I manage a smile.

"Well, I'm also really perceptive."

"Not to mention incredibly modest," I reply.

Laughter comes easily to us again, and something about the way he's considering me across the table makes me think it surprises him as much as it surprises me.

"I am perceptive, though." Grip takes one of the last bites of his burger. "Like your face when Skeet—"

"Dropped the N-word in front of me like it was nothing?" I cut in, knowing exactly where he's going. "Yeah, like what's up with that? I don't understand anyone being okay with that word."

Grip looks at me for a moment before shuttering his eyes, shrugging, and picking up one of his last fries.

"Probably because to him it *is* nothing. I mean, if he says it. If we say it."

"But I couldn't say it, right?" I clarify unnecessarily.

He holds a French fry suspended mid-way to his mouth. "Do you want to say it?" He considers me carefully.

"God, no." My gasp is worthy of a Victorian novel. "Of course not."

"You can tell me." He leans forward, his eyes teasing me conspiratorially. "Not even when you're singing along to the hippity hop and they say it?"

"We've already established that I don't listen to the hippity hop very much," I say wryly.

This is such a sensitive topic, one I'd hesitate to approach with people I know well, much less someone I just met. In conversations like these, before we say our words, they're ammunition. After we've said them, they're smoking bullets. There seems to be no middle ground and too little common ground for dialogue to be productive. We just tiptoe around things, afraid we'll offend or look ignorant, be misunderstood. Honesty is a risk few are willing to take. For some reason, it's a risk I decide to take with Grip.

"I just mean, isn't that a double standard?" I pause to sift through my thoughts and get this question right. "It's such an incendiary word with such an awful history. I completely understand why Black people wouldn't be okay with it at all."

"Well, then you're halfway there."

I shoot him a look from under my lashes, trying to gauge before I go any further if he thinks I'm some weird, entitled white girl asking dumb questions, which I probably am. He's just waiting, though, eyes intent and clear of mockery or judgment.

"So why . ..why should anyone use it? Why put it in songs? Why does Skeet feel okay calling another Black man that?"

"First of all, I'm not one of those people who assumes because I'm Black, I somehow represent every Black person's perspective," Grip says. "So, I'll just tell you how I and the people I'm around most think about it."

He pauses and then laughs a little.

"I guess we don't think about it. It's such a natural part of how we interact with each other." He gives me a wry smile. "Some of us feel like we take the power away from it when we use it."

"Taking the power?" I shake my head, fascinated, but confused. "What does that mean?"

"Like we get to determine how it's used."

He pauses, and I can almost see him weighing the words before they leave his mouth.

"You have to account for intent. It was originally meant to degrade and dehumanize, as a weapon against us, but we reappropriate it as ours and get to use it as we see fit."

"I don't know that I really get that or agree," I admit, hesitant because I've been misunderstood before in these conversations. I'm too curious. I always want to understand, and don't always know when to stop asking.

"Because of our unique history in this country, that word will never be safe for anyone to use to us," he says quietly. "But with all that Black people endured, being able to take that slur back and decide how we want to use it feels like the least we should be allowed. And it's the very definition of entitlement for others to want to use it because we can."

"That I get." I hesitate, wanting to respect his opinion, his honesty even though I don't agree with parts of what he's said. "I guess to me, we have enough that divides us and makes us misunderstand each other. Do we really need one more thing we can't agree on?"

Grip's eyes don't waver from my face, but it's as if he's not as much looking at me, as absorbing what I just said. Processing it.

"That's actually a great point," he says after a few seconds. "I hadn't thought of it like that, and it's good that you ask that question. You're not asking the wrong question. Is it the most important question, though? To me, some guy calls me the N-word, we'll probably fight. I'll kick his ass, and we're done. It's over."

He slants me a cocky grin, and my lips refuse not to smile back. "But I want to hear the same dismay and curiosity," he continues, his smile leveling out. "About the issues that are actually eroding our communities. Let's ask why Black men are six percent of the general population and nearly forty percent of the prison population. Let's get some outrage over people of color getting longer sentences for the same crimes other people commit. And over disproportionate unemployment and poverty."

His handsome face settles into a plane of sharp angles, bold lines, and indignation.

"I can fight a dude who calls me the N-word," he says. "It's harder to fight a whole system stacked against me."

The passion and conviction coming off him in waves cannon across the table and land on my chest, ratcheting up my heartbeat.

"It's not bad that you ask why we call each other that, Bristol." The sharp lines of his face soften. "There's just bigger issues that actually affect our lives, our futures, our children, and that's what we want to talk about."

Nothing in his eyes makes me feel guilty for asking, and I think that he wants me to understand as much as I want to.

"When other people are as outraged and as curious about those problems as Black people are," he says, "then maybe we can solve them together."

It's quiet for a few moments as we absorb each other's perspectives. My mind feels stretched. As if someone, this man, took the edges of my thoughts and pulled them in new directions, to new proportions.

"Now that I get," I finally say softly. "You're right. Those things are more important, and that's powerful."

I look up and grin to lighten the moment.

"But don't think you've changed my mind about the N-word. That still doesn't make sense to me."

He leans forward with a wide smile, his eyes alive and dark and bright all at once. And I wonder if this is the most stimulating conversation he's had in a long time. It is for me.

"Is there anything that you don't completely know how it works or why it works, but you know the rules that govern it?" he asks.

"Um, Twitter?" I laugh, glad when he responds with a smile. "Then the N-word is your Twitter."

He sits back in his seat, long legs stretched under the table, arms spread on the back of the booth, and a smile in his eyes for me.

"You may have me halfway to understanding that," I say. "But you will not get me to be okay with the misogyny that is such a part of hip-hop culture."

"I don't disrespect women in my lyrics," he says immediately. "My mom would kill me."

"Well, maybe I'll listen to some of your stuff."

"I feel honored that you would deign to listen to my music."

I toss a napkin across the table at him, and it bounces harmlessly off his face. He throws it back at me and laughs.

"I mean, for real," he says. "What kind of self-respecting, white millennial doesn't listen to hip-hop?"

He laughs when I roll my eyes at him.

"Are you one of those people who thinks hip-hop belongs to Black people?" I ask.

"Of course it does." He smooths the humor from his expression. "We made it. It's ours in the same way jazz and the blues and R&B are ours. We innovated, making sound where there was no sound before. The very roots of hip-hop are in West Africa from centuries ago. But we share our shit all the time, so you're welcome."

I lift a brow at his ethno-arrogance, but he throws his head back laughing at me, maybe at himself.

"Art, specifically music, is a living thing," he says. "It isn't just absorbed by the people who hear it, but it absorbs them. So, we shared hip-hop with the world, and it isn't just ours anymore. The Beastie Boys heard it. Eminem heard it. Whoever heard it fell in love with it, added to it, and became a part of it."

"And that's a good thing?"

"Mostly. If that hadn't happened, if we hadn't shared it and someone other than us loved it, it'd still be niche. Underground. Now it's global, but that wouldn't have happened if it hadn't gone mainstream. Mainstream means more opportunities, so I'm all for white, Asian, Hispanic. We need everybody buying hip-hop, because ultimately, it's about that green."

He rubs imaginary dollars between his fingers before going on.

"I think some fear that when hip-hop goes mainstream, it's mixed with other influences. It's diluted, and I get that, but we have to evolve. That isn't selling out. That's survival."

The way he talks about music and art fascinates me. Rhyson's talent, his genius, always isolated him from me. I've been around musicians all my life, but with no talent of my own, I was always on the outside and couldn't figure out how to get in. Grip just shared that with me. He let me in.

Before I can dig anymore, Jimmi takes the stage for her performance. And when I say she takes the stage, she takes it. She owns it.

She overpowers the small space, and you know she's something special.

"Wow." I spoon into the fudge brownie and ice cream I ordered during Jimmi's set. "She can back those tits up, huh?"

"She definitely can," Grip says. "And speaking of double standards, I think you have one criticizing hip-hop for its misogyny and then hating on another woman just because she has a great rack. Is it any worse when men judge women's worth by their looks than when women do it?"

He's serious. At first, I think he's joking, but then I realize his eyes hold a subtle rebuke. He's protective of Jimmi. Maybe they're together? The thought sours the ice cream in my mouth, and it shouldn't. I've known this guy for all of a couple hours. And he isn't my type. And I'm leaving in a week.

"I wasn't judging her."

His look and the twist of his lips say otherwise.

"Okay, maybe I was judging her a little bit." I laugh and am glad when he laughs, too. "She's a pretty girl, and sometimes they get a bad rap."

"They?" Grip lifts his thick brows. "Do you not realize how beautiful you are?"

I have no idea how to respond. I'm attractive. I know that. Guys have been hitting on me since middle school.

"Whatever." I shrug. "I just don't define myself by my looks. There's a lot more to me than that."

"I believe you," Grip says. "I'm just saying there's a lot more to Jimmi, too, so maybe you guys have a lot in common. And maybe you should withhold judgment until you know her better. If not altogether."

I'm quiet while I finish my brownie and think about what he said. He has a point. One I hadn't considered. I had to leave my Ivy League college to get the most thought-provoking, stimulating conversation I've had in ages. Maybe ever. And with a rapper. Jimmi isn't the only one there's more to than meets the eye.

4

GRIP

I FIGURED RHYSON'S sister would be attractive. I mean, they're twins, and he's one of those guys girls trip all over themselves for. And I knew she went to an Ivy League college, so of course she's smart. But Bristol is all kinds of things I could not have anticipated or prepared for. Her curiosity, her authenticity, and her honesty hook something in me and draw me closer. I didn't expect the conversation we had at Mick's to go where it did. I loved that she wasn't afraid to wade through the difficult questions of race, and that she gave measured, thoughtful responses and expected the same from me. Those are tough conversations to have with someone you know, much less with someone you just met, but it felt like nothing was off-limits. As if I could give her room to be naïve and she could give me room to be obnoxious. We both gave each other space to be misunderstood, because we really wanted to understand.

I admit only to myself that I'm drawn to her in a way that is dangerous because she's Rhyson's sister. Starting something that can't go anywhere could be awkward down the road. I'm not that guy.

Usually I fuck them and then I leave them. That's it. That's all. And I can't do that to Rhyson's sister.

The string of text messages reminds me there's a girl I'm trying to leave even now. I've been dating Tessa for two months, but we haven't really talked in the last couple of weeks. She blew my mind the first time we had sex, and her pussy put some kind of hex on me and made me agree to "dating." Well, that hex has worn off. I told her we probably need to take a break, but she either wasn't hearing me or was ignoring me. When I tell a girl we need to take a break, that's code for there's this other chick I'm feeling so we should cut this off before I do something we'll both regret. I wish I could just let it fade, but I'm going to have to actually break it off. She keeps hitting me up, so it seems like that conversation will have to happen soon.

I steal a glance across at Bristol, who's slumped in the passenger seat with her head dropped to an awkward angle while she sleeps. She probably wouldn't give me the time of day anyway. Rhyson's so unassuming that you'd never know he comes from deep pockets. Old money and new. He turned his back on that life to emancipate from his parents, but Bristol still occupies that world. A guy like me, driving this piece of shit Jeep, sweeping floors, and doing odd jobs to make ends meet—no way would she check for me. She doesn't even listen to hip-hop. She probably hasn't ever dated a Black guy, and I wouldn't be the exception.

Now me? I like to think of myself as an equal opportunity connoisseur. My dick is not so much color blind, as it loves every color. And I have a rainbow coalition fuck record to prove it. If it's wet and tight, I don't really care what color it is.

Crude, I know.

Maybe that's an issue of race I won't explore with Bristol. I'm sure she has her limits.

I pull up in front of my apartment complex. I'm kind of glad Bristol's asleep. Maybe I can sneak inside and get back out to the car before she wakes up. I need to grab my laptop for the tracks I'll work on while I'm at Grady's. I wouldn't have stopped otherwise. We joked at the airport about her suitcase being bigger than my apartment. She isn't far off.

I'm carefully, quietly opening the driver side door when she stirs.

"Hey." She sits up and stretches her arms over her head, straining the tank top against her breasts. "Where are you going?"

My mouth goes dry when her nipples pucker through the thin material. I can resist her for my best friend. Bristol and Rhyson may not be close, but she is still his sister. A pretty face and a great set of tits aren't worth any possible static with him. I may need to sticky note that over my mirror this week, though.

"Oh, you're up." I lean through the window. "I just need to run inside my apartment and grab something before we head to Grady's."

"Can I use your bathroom?"

Shit. I mentally run through the disaster area that is my tiny apartment. I'll be lucky if a roach doesn't greet us at the door.

"Um, sure. Come on."

When we cross the landing, I remind myself I have nothing to be ashamed of. I pay my rent. I'm making my own way and not breaking any laws. I have the integrity of my art, not selling out for the quick buck, but holding out for the right opportunity. It all sounds hollow when Bristol, in her lambskin leather and designer distressed jeans, blows into my one-room apartment on a cloud of expensive perfume.

"Through there." I point to the tiny bathroom off the one room that encompasses the kitchen, living room, and bedroom. The brochure called it "studio," but hovel is probably a more accurate description.

Bristol's sharp eyes wander over the threadbare thrift store couch and the Dollar Store dishes in the drying rack. The disarray of my narrow, unmade bed, which is flush against a wall, mocks me.

"Could you hurry up?" I ask curtly. "We need to get going."

Her startled eyes stare back at me for a moment before she moves quickly to the bathroom. I grab my laptop and am already standing by the door when she comes out.

"There wasn't a towel." She holds up her dripping hands.

"Oh, sorry." I take the few strides to the kitchen and grab a roll of paper towels on the counter for her.

She dries her hands and tosses the used paper towels into the trash. Instead of following me back to the door, she leans against the counter.

"I thought you were tired." I shift from one foot to the other, back propping the door open. "Let's go."

"I have that same print." She nods to the poster of Nina Simone hanging on the wall over my bed. "She was an excellent pianist, and my mother loves her."

My shoulders, which have been tight since we pulled up in front of my dump apartment, relax an inch.

"Yeah?" is my only response.

Bristol nods and walks over to my turntable against the far wall, running her fingers over the dust cover. "You use this to deejay?"

I'm standing here holding the door open for her to leave, and she's conducting an inspection.

"Uh, yeah."

"You're still deejaying tomorrow at that place Jimmi was talking about?" She looks up from the turntable, apparently in no hurry to leave. "Brew?"

"Yeah, that's what I'll use for some of the set. I prefer vinyl, but most setups nowadays are completely digital." I sigh and nod my head out to the hall. "Look, we better get going."

"What's the hurry? Rhyson's at the studio and Grady's at his retreat all week. Just an empty house waiting for us."

"I'm ready to go. I have better things to do than give a perfect stranger a grand tour of my place when I need to be working."

Hurt strikes through her eyes so quickly, I almost miss it. She lowers her lashes and walks toward me without addressing my rudeness. She's squeezing past me in the doorway when my conscience reprimands me. I grab her elbow to stop her from leaving, tucking her into the doorway, too.

"Hey." My hand slides down her arm to take her hand. "I'm sorry."

I'm an asshole. I didn't mean to snap at you. I don't know why I did that."

She looks up at me, her back against one side of the doorframe, mine against the other. With her coming where she's from, and me coming from where I'm from, there should be a vast ocean separating us, filled with our differences and all the reasons we should never meet on shore. But there's only this wedge of charged space between our bodies that seems to be shrinking by the second. What should be foreign feels familiar. When I assume I know something, she surprises me.

"You have nothing to be ashamed of," she says softly. "I'm sorry I made that crack at the airport about my suitcase being bigger than your apartment. "

"I actually said that," I remind her, pulling up a smile from somewhere.

"Whatever." She waves a dismissive hand, grinning just the smallest bit in return. "My point is that I'm a spoiled bitch sometimes. I can't blame you for assuming I would judge your place. I just want you to know that I don't. Hearing all the things you do on the side so you can pursue your craft, I admire that kind of commitment."

"Thank you." I look at her, cataloging her features one by one and realizing the most fascinating thing about this girl isn't visible to the naked eye.

"When you're rich and famous, you'll look back on this time—this apartment—and laugh. And appreciate how far you've gone."

"You haven't even heard my stuff." I scoff and smile. "How do you know I'll be successful?"

"My brother's a genius. You must be talented or he wouldn't make time for you." Her lips twist just the slightest bit. "Believe me, I know from personal experience how little time Rhyson has for the mediocre."

"So you don't sing or play?"

Her face lights up with genuine humor.

"Much to the dismay of all my music instructors. Everyone thought they'd get a female version of Rhyson."

"And you . . ." I lift my brows, waiting for her to tell me what they got.

"Can't carry a tune in a bucket or a note in my pocket to save my life," she says. "I tried the clarinet, and was only ... I think the word my instructor used to describe me was 'adequate.'"

"It can't be that bad. I mean, Grady and Rhyson are both obviously incredible musicians. Your parents played themselves, didn't they, before they started managing?"

"Yes, they all play, which makes me the ugly duckling."

I don't even realize that my hand has lifted to brush my knuckle across the slant of her cheekbone until it's done. Her eyes widen, but she doesn't pull away. Her skin is like warm silk to touch.

"Ugly? I doubt that." My voice comes out all deep and husky. If I keep this up, I'll be excusing myself to jerk off in the tiny bathroom. "We better go."

I drop my hand from her face and clear my throat. I need to stay focused, not on her face and body and that clever brain, but on getting out of here without spreading her out on my unmade bed.

5

BRISTOL

I'VE READ THE same line several times. My laptop could be upside down and I probably wouldn't notice. I'm sitting here on the couch with my computer propped on my knees, not making any headway on the essay for my internship application. I could blame fatigue considering I haven't really stopped since I left New York this morning. And my body clock may still be on East Coast. And I am getting hungry again. I could use those excuses for my lack of focus, but there's only one real reason if I'm honest.

Grip.

He's an unexpected fascination, a tantalizing riddle I keep turning over in my head. I keep hoping he'll make sense eventually, but then I'm somehow glad he doesn't add up or behave the way I think he should.

If he were in the same room, I'd still be surreptitiously gawking, stealing glances at one of the most beautiful men I've ever seen, but he's in Grady's music room working on his own stuff. He went there almost immediately after we arrived, and I haven't heard a peep from him since. I guess he is as obsessed with music as my brother. Yet another reason not to venture too deeply into the attraction I feel for him.

"Not that he's here," I mumble. "He isn't much company."

I'm the one who said he doesn't have to keep me company, and now I'm complaining because he isn't. Maybe I imagined the charged moment at his apartment in the doorway. He touched my cheek. It was barely a brush of his fingers over my face, but it ignited . . .something. Emotion? Desire? I'm not sure, but I haven't felt it before. Based on what I've seen of the player and his "chocolate charm," I shouldn't be feeling anything at all if I know what's good for me.

I learned early on that people aren't careful with your emotions. They're too self-involved to consider how their actions affect others. I saw it when my parents forced Rhyson to tour, even though it was ripping our family apart. I've seen it in Rhyson's own disregard for our relationship and how easy it was for him to walk away, forgetting he had a twin sister on the other side of the country. I've seen it in my parents' sham of a marriage. They're partners, but I'm not sure they genuinely care for one another at all. Certainly there isn't any love. I protect my heart because no one else will.

Sometimes I wish I didn't have a heart at all because, despite knowing what I know, I keep putting it out there to my family. Here I am, visiting Rhyson and willing to move after graduation if he'll have me. I used to be afraid I'd be like my parents, careless. Now, I fear that I care too much about people who don't give a damn.

"Machiavelli?" Grip's voice, as deep and rich as espresso, caresses the nape of my neck from behind, making me jump. "Interesting choice."

I look from the sharply hewn lines of his face to the flashing cursor behind Machiavelli's name on my screen.

"Sorry." He walks around to sit beside me on the couch. "Didn't mean to startle you."

I set my laptop on the coffee table and scoot a few inches away, tucking myself into the corner of the couch. I wasn't doing a good job focusing when he was in the other room. With the breadth of his shoulders, the stretch of his muscular legs, and the towering energy he brought with him, I give up. I'll work on it tomorrow. A thrill passes through me at the prospect of another conversation with him. I'm not one of those giddy girls who gets all breathless when a guy comes around. And yet, with those caramel-colored eyes resting on my face, I'm short of breath.

"Isn't this spring break?" Grip crooks a grin at me and leans into the opposite corner of the couch. "Seems like even Ivy League should get some time off."

"Oh, I'm taking some time off for sure." I tuck my legs under me.

Since I exchanged my jeans for some old cut-offs, I have to pretend not to notice him looking a little too long at my bare legs. The last thing I need is to get the idea that he likes me.

"So, you write essays about Machiavelli to relax?"

"Not exactly." I laugh and scoop my hair up into a topknot. "I'm applying for an internship. The application is due next week, and I need to finish the essay."

"What's the essay on?"

"I have to write about an icon of power from history."

"And you chose Machiavelli?" He chuckles, considering me from beneath the long curl of his lashes. "Remind me not to get on your bad side."

"You know much about him?"

He pulls his T-shirt up from the hem, and my heart pops an artery or something because it shouldn't be working this hard while at rest. I swallow hard at the layer of muscle wrapped around his ribs. One pectoral muscle peeks from under the shirt, tipped with the dark disc of his nipple. My mouth literally waters, and I can't think beyond pulling it between my lips and suckling him. Hard.

"Do you see it?" he asks.

"Huh?" I reluctantly drag my eyes from the ladder of velvet-covered muscle and sinew to the expectant look on his face. "See what?"

"The tattoo." He runs a finger over the ink scrawled across his ribs.

Makavelli.

"I hate to break it to you," I say with a smirk. "But someone stuck you with a permanent typo."

He laughs, dropping the shirt, which is really a shame because I was just learning to breathe with all that masculine beauty on display.

"Bristol, stop playing. You know it's on purpose, right?"

"Oh, sure, it is, Grip." I roll my eyes. "Nice try."

"Are you serious?" He looks at me like I'm from outer space. "You know that's how Tupac referred to himself on his posthumous album, right? That he misspelled it on purpose?"

I clear my throat and scratch at an imaginary itch on the back of my neck.

"Um ... yes?"

His warm laughter at my expense washes over me, and it's worth being the butt of the joke, because I get to see his face animated. He's even more handsome when he laughs.

"You're funny." He laughs again, more softly this time. "I didn't expect that."

"Why not?" I frown. "Did Rhyson make me sound like I wasn't any fun?"

"He hasn't said much at all, actually."

I figured I wasn't paramount in his mind, but it hurts to hear how little Rhyson has told his friends about me. Even when I resented my parents lavishing all their attention and love on my brother, I was proud of him. I told anyone who would listen about how talented he was. How he traveled all over the world. I wanted everyone to know. Again, my heart is a scale out of balance, with my end taking all the weight.

"I didn't mean it that way," Grip says after a moment of my silence. "I can tell you and Rhyson have a lot to work out."

"If he ever comes home, I'm sure we will." I search for something to shift the attention again. "So, you're a Tupac fan?"

"That would be an understatement. Fanatic is more like it."

"Even I know the Biggie–Tupac debate," I say with a slight smile. "I guess I don't have to ask where you fall."

"Oh, Pac, all day, every day." Grip's passion for the subject lights his eyes. "I mean, I give Biggie his props, but Pac was a poet, and truly had something to say. He was unflinchingly honest in his commentary on social justice and the state of his community. He was brilliant."

"You don't talk like most rappers I know." I smile because I hear how bad it sounds, but I somehow feel like I can say it to him even ineloquently.

"And we've already established that you know so many rappers." He crosses his arms over his chest, the cut of his muscles flexing with the movement. "Some of your best friends are rappers. You're so down."

His dark eyes glint with humor.

"Don't make fun of me." I fake pout.

"But it's so much fun." He fake pouts back. "I meant it as a compliment."

"Yes, but by comparison it would be an insult to other rappers, right?" He's half-teasing, half-challenging.

"I don't enjoy this logic thing you're doing. It's making me seem narrow-minded."

"If the mind fits," he comes back with a smirk.

"I should be irritated with you for calling me out." I try to keep my face stern.

"And I should be disgusted by your preconceived notions." He glances up from under his long lashes, his mouth relaxed, not quite smiling. "But I'm not."

"And why is that?" I ask softly, my breath held hostage by the look in his eyes under hooded lids. I want to look away. I should, but he should first, and he doesn't. So we're both trapped in a moment, unsure of how to do the thing we should do. When I feel like my nerves will snap from the heated tension, he clears his throat.

"Um, I thought you might be getting hungry again." He stands without answering my question, running both hands over the closely cut wave of his hair. "Wanna order something? Pizza? Thai?"

"Anybody do good empanadas around here?"

"You kidding me?" He pulls out his phone and smiles. "This is LA. If there's anything we have, it's good Mexican."

We order and are eating in Grady's kitchen within the hour. I sip the beer he grabbed from Grady's refrigerator.

"This is good."

"So you like Mexican," he says.

"Empanadas especially." I eye the last one in the Styrofoam tray on the marble island centered in Grady's kitchen.

"The way you're looking at that empanada is very *Lord of the Flies*. Like I might have to fight you for it. Like it's the conch."

"So are you Piggy in this analogy?" I pour false indignation into my voice and prop my fists on my hips.

"I ain't Jack."

I snatch the last empanada before he has a chance to, and he throws his head back laughing, shoulders shaking.

"To be so skinny, you put it away," he says once he's finished laughing at me.

"Skinny?" I glance at my legs in the cut-offs. "I'm not skinny."

"Okay, do you prefer slim?"

"I guess you're all 'I like big butts and I cannot lie.'"

"You know, that's the only hip-hop reference you've gotten right all day, and it's from like ninety-two."

"That's not fair." I clear away the cartons and paper from our delivery meal. "If I ask you about songs I like, you probably wouldn't know them, either."

"Wrong. I would shut you down." He takes his phone out of his pocket and puts it on the counter. "Check my playlists."

I look at him for an extra few seconds, and he tips his head in invitation toward the phone.

"Go for it."

I sigh but grab his phone and scroll through his songs. Coldplay,

Alanis Morissette, Jay Z, Usher, Justin Timberlake, Lil Wayne, U2, Talib Kweli, Jill Scott.

"Carrie Underwood?" I glance up from his phone to meet his wide grin.

"First of all, the girl's fine as hell. Second of all, who doesn't like 'Jesus, Take the Wheel'?"

"Oh, my God! You're ridiculous."

"We've talked a lot about my musical tastes today, but not about yours. I showed you mine, now show me yours."

I will not think about him showing me his. I wonder, not for the first time today, if I packed my good vibrators.

"Let's just say my playlist would be a lot less varied," I offer, dissembling all thoughts of the muscular physique hidden beneath his clothes.

"White bread, huh?" His knowing smile should irritate me, but I find myself answering with one of my own.

"And what would you call yours?"

"Multi-grain."

I shake my head, dispose of the trash, and head back into the living room. I sit on the couch but don't make a move to pick up my laptop. When I look up, there's uncertainty on his face.

"Are you gonna work or . . ." His question dangles in the air waiting for me to catch it.

"No, someone told me even Ivy League should relax on spring break."

He laughs and takes his spot in the opposite corner of the couch. "Rhyson should be home soon," he says.

I'd almost forgotten to be irritated with my brother. Grip does a great job distracting me.

"It'll be good to see him again." I sit cross-legged on the couch and palm my knees. "I'm glad he found you guys out here. He needed somebody in his life."

"We're as close as brothers," Grip says softly. "I probably wouldn't have made it through those first few years of high school without him. That school was like a foreign country."

"Was it so different from your old one?"

"Uh, night and day. Growing up in Compton is no joke." The quick-to-smile curve of his lips settles into a sober line. "The School of the Arts required a completely different set of survival skills. I've learned to navigate any world I find myself in. Be whatever I need to be for every situation."

"You adapted?"

"Had to. Constantly." Grip chuckles just a little. "It was tough, but it taught me to be comfortable, even in environments where there's no one else like me. I got whiplash trying to be one thing at school and another thing at home with my friends and family."

He shrugs.

"So I just decided to be myself. To adapt, yeah, but never lose who I am."

"That's cool," I say. "It took me longer to figure that out. Sometimes I think I still am."

We both tuck our private thoughts into the silence that follows my confession.

"Well, being myself comes and goes." Grip gives me a smile that takes some of the heaviness out of the room. "We're always tempted to be something else when it's easier. My mom was determined for me to go to that school, but she always challenged me to stay true to who I was."

"It's just the two of you?"

"Yeah, always has been." He leans forward, elbows on knees as he speaks. "She is the single most influential force in my life. She demanded so much from me. Wanted more for me than most guys from my neighborhood end up having."

"Sounds like you guys are really close."

"We are. When my teacher realized I could write, she pushed for the scholarship. If it were left to me, I never would have tried. I didn't want to leave my friends and go to a school across town with a bunch of rich, uppity kids. That was how I thought of it then."

He glances up from the floor, his eyes crinkling at the corners.

"My mom dragged me up to that school for the entry exams and sat there while I took every test."

My mother probably never even knew one of my teachers' names in school. I'm the "privileged" one, considering our wealth growing up, but I feel positively deprived as Grip talks about the active role his mother took in his upbringing, in his life.

"She used to give me a supplemental book list every school year. Books she said the schools wouldn't teach. She said, 'Don't wait for nobody to give you nothing. Even your education you have to take. If the one they offer you isn't enough, make your own.'"

"Is that how you're so well-read? Or at least seem to be." I raise my brows at him. "Or maybe that's just how you pick up the smart girls?"

"Are you a smart girl, Bristol?" His voice fondles my name.

"You can't turn off the flirt, can you?" I ask to distract myself from the fact that it's working.

"Was I flirting?" He lifts one brow. "I wasn't trying to. I wasn't gonna bother because I assumed you weren't into the brothers."

A puff of air gets trapped in my throat as I try to draw a deep breath. I cough, aware of his eyes on me the whole time.

"That isn't how I decide who I'm 'into', as you call it," I say once I've cleared my airway.

"You telling me you've dated a Black guy before?" Surprise colors the look he gives me. Surprise and something else. Something warmer.

I wish I could surprise him, but I can't.

"No, I've never dated a Black guy." An imp prompts my next comment. "What am I missing?"

The warmth overtakes the surprise in his eyes, spiking to a simmer that heats the gold in his brown eyes molten.

"Oh, you don't want to know." Grip's voice goes a shade darker. "It might spoil you for all the others."

"You think so?" A sensual tension sifts into the air between us. "They say once you go Black." He stretches out his smile. "You won't go back."

A laugh pops out of my mouth before I can check it. "And that's your experience? Have you been disappointed by the rest of the female rainbow?"

My pulse slows while I wait for him to respond, like if my heart hammers I might miss an inflection in his voice. He puts me on high alert.

"Oh, no. By no means." Grip leans back, considering me from under heavy eyelids. "I don't care what color a girl is. I like the color of smart, the shade of funny, and sexy is my favorite hue."

"If that isn't a line, then I don't know what it is," I scoff, but his words tie a band around my chest that makes it harder to breathe.

"I'm not wasting my lines on you. You're the kind of girl who wouldn't respond to bullshit anyway."

He assesses me shrewdly, and for a moment, I feel like he's pushed up under my shell, insinuated himself under my skin to see the very bones no one has ever been privy to.

"So what color am I then?" I ask before thinking better of it. He'll probably just say I'm white, obviously.

"What color are you?" he repeats, his eyes never leaving my face. "You, Bristol, are a freaking prism."

6

GRIP

I NEED TO put the brakes on this.

It's one thing to be secretly attracted to Rhyson's sister. It's another thing altogether to encourage her attraction to me.

And Bristol is attracted to me.

I know when a girl wants a taste. Some girls I look at and immediately know they're slurpers. They'll eat the soup and tip the bowl up, slurping greedily till the last drop. Bristol ... she would eat you slowly, savor you in delicate bites until there's nothing left of you but an empty plate. And then she would lick her fingers. She's very sensual. It's subtle, but I notice these things. The way she lifted her hair off her neck at lunch today to feel the ocean breeze. The way she explored the ridges of the empanada with her tongue before taking a bite, groaning when the flavors flooded her mouth. Her body seeks sensation, presses in to discover what the world offers to stimulate her. I don't think she knows it about herself, and it's a shame some man hasn't taught her, but I can't be that guy.

Though, I'd make an excellent instructor.

For the second time today, I find myself watching her sleep. I don't watch chicks sleep, not even after I fuck them. It's usually more of a ... dilemma. More like ... well, this is awkward. I really don't want her to stay, but she fell asleep. My dick put her into a semi-coma, so I should at least let her sleep it off. That kind of thing. Certainly not noticing how her eyelashes make half-moon shadows on her cheeks. Or the satiny texture of her skin. Or the constellation of almost indiscernible freckles splattered across her nose because she was out in the sun today. I certainly wouldn't be wondering if somehow she might be dreaming about me.

We talked. That's the problem with this girl. She doesn't just talk. She probes. She ponders. She wonders. She asks. She carries on a helluva conversation, which from my experience, is a lost art. We talked about our childhoods, high school, our aspirations, and our dreams. My favorite show of all time, *The Wire*. Her favorite show of all time, *West Wing*. How neither of us has ever seen *How I Met Your Mother*, and don't understand *Two and a Half Men*. She can't believe I've never seen *Swingers*. I can't believe she's never seen *Purple Rain*. We talked about things we don't understand and aren't sure we ever will. Things we thought we had figured out, only to realize we didn't know jack shit. It feels fresh like a beginning, but it also feels like we've known each other for years.

It's two o'clock in the morning, and her body's on East Coast, so of course, she eventually succumbed to exhaustion, but even then, she fought it, drifting off mid-sentence. And dammit, if I don't want to wake her up and ask what she was about to say.

This is bad.

This is really bad.

The garage door opening snaps me out of my own tangled thoughts. I get up from the couch, moving as quietly as I can so I don't wake her. Rhyson's coming through the garage door just as I enter the kitchen. Fatigue sketches lines around his mouth. His eyes are dulled by all the day behind him and the non-stop work it involved.

"Dude." He walks over and daps me up before slumping into one of the high stools at the kitchen island. "Shitty, shitty day. These execs don't know what they want, and don't know what they don't want until you've spent hours making it. Anyway, thanks for picking up Bristol and taking care of her today."

"No problem." I lean against the wall, noting all the similarities between his face and Bristol's. I was struck by how alike they are in other ways, too. Rhyson and I also connected right away when we were both new guys. I shouldn't be surprised to feel a quick and deep connection with his twin sister, but I still am.

"Where is she?" Rhyson gets up to open the refrigerator, staring at its contents for a few seconds before turning to face me.

"In the living room." I tip my head in that direction. "Knocked out."

"On that couch? She'll regret it in the morning. I'll get her to the guest room."

He closes the fridge and sits down again. I can't tell if it's nerves about seeing his sister after so long, or that frenetic energy we feel after being immersed in our music for so long. You're exhausted, but you're on this high and can't settle right away.

"Yeah, she was pretty tired," I say. "We had lunch at Mick's."

"For real?" Rhyson glances up, a slight quirk to his lips. "How's Jim?"

"Still feeling you." I roll my eyes but have to laugh. She's been into Rhyson since tenth grade, but he's never given her the time of day.

"Not gonna happen." He shakes his head for emphasis. "We're such good friends. Why does she want to spoil it with fucking?"

"I usually like it when girls 'spoil' things with fucking." We both laugh at my half-joke. "But in Jimmi's case, I know what you mean. Just friends."

"Right, and that isn't changing." Rhyson runs his hands through his already-disheveled hair. "How is she? My sister, I mean?"

"Go see for yourself," I say. "When was the last time you saw her?"

"Four, five years," Rhyson mumbles, sliding his glance to the side, not so much, it seems, to avoid my eyes as to avoid something inside himself.

"Man, how'd you go that long without seeing your twin sister?"
"You know how things went down with my parents after I emancipated." Defensiveness stiffens his voice and his back.

"Your parents, Rhys, not your sister."

"Same thing." Rhyson's shrug is supposed to look careless, but it
doesn't. He cares. "She's been under their roof all this time. She's
probably just like my mother."

The girl I spent the day with is nothing like the she-dragon
Rhyson described his mother to be.

"Maybe she isn't," I say. "Or maybe you never spent enough time
with her to know her in the first place."

"Is that what she told you?" Rhyson narrows his eyes. "If we didn't
spend time together, it wasn't my fault. She got to go to school and
parties and shop and have friends. Be normal. Do whatever the hell
she wanted while my parents tracked my every step, dragging me all
over the world like a show pony."

"I just can't imagine not seeing my family for that long, at least
not my sister, if I had one, much less my twin sister."

"Yeah, but you've got your mom and Jade and your aunts. You
have a normal family. I've got the Borgias."

"Normal?" A snort of disbelieving air whooshes past my lips. "I'm
pretty sure my Uncle Jamal was a real life pimp at some point."

"Dude, you may be right." Humor lightens his expression for the
first time since he came through the garage door.

"Seriously! You'd get arrested doing half the stuff he tells you to
do to girls."

We laugh, recalling all the slightly disturbing advice my uncle
often dispenses about women.

"Okay, so maybe your family isn't completely normal," he
concedes. "But you have to admit, mine is the freak show that
everyone had tickets to."

Even before I met Rhyson, I'd seen the news about the courtroom
battle he endured to emancipate from his parents. The sensational-
ized details were inescapable, plastered on the front page of every
tabloid for weeks.

"I just don't know what she wants from me," Rhyson says softly, his eyes unfocused as if he's asking himself.

"I think she wants her brother back."

I straighten from the wall and walk over to join him at the counter so I can talk softer in case she wakes up and hears.

"Seems like she's missed you," I say in a low tone, looking at him intently. "She seems hurt that you let it go this long and haven't been really responsive when she reached out before."

"I just didn't know where she stood," Rhyson says. "Battle lines were drawn, and I thought she took my parents' side. To survive, I had to distance myself from everything associated with them."

Rhyson looks haunted for a moment, like he's seen a ghost. I know the ghost is actually himself when he first left home, addicted to prescription drugs and barely able to function.

"Maybe you should just tell her that," I say. "Maybe that's the quickest way to a fresh start."

"Maybe." Rhyson rolls his shoulders and sighs. "So, what's she look like?"

Beautiful.

"Um ... good," I say instead, clearing my throat and dropping my eyes to study the swirling pattern in the countertop. "She looks good."

It's so quiet that I finally look up to find Rhyson staring a burning hole through my forehead. We know each other too well.

"She's my sister, Marlon." A warning lights his eyes. "Don't mess with her. None of that chocolate charm shit you put on these other unsuspecting girls."

"I wouldn't." I steel my voice against the doubt I have even in myself. I should be able to leave Bristol alone, but after today, I'm not sure that I will. But I'm not admitting that to my best friend until I absolutely have to.

"Not that I have to worry about you since you're"—he throws up air quotes—"'taken'. Aren't you and Tessa still a thing?"

I just shrug, too tired to discuss the complication of disentangling myself from Tessa.

"Not for much longer," I settle for saying and leave it at that.

When we go back into the living room, Bristol's in the same spot as when I left her. She's pulled her knees under her and tucked her hands under the cheek laid against the couch. I draped a blanket over her, but it's slipped some, leaving visible her face, the slim shoulders in her tank top, all the dark and burnished hair falling down her back, tendrils clinging to her neck.

Rhyson gapes like he's never seen her before. If that picture was anything to go by, I guess she's changed a lot in five years. He approaches her with slow steps and then squats down by the couch. He stretches his hand toward her hair but then hesitates, dropping it back down to his side. A muscle knots at his jawline, and his lips clamp tight. He blinks rapidly and swallows whatever emotions he doesn't want her to see when she wakes up.

"Bristol," he says softly, shaking her shoulder. "Wake up."

Her eyes open slowly, lashes fluttering over her cheeks for a few seconds. She turns her head to see who woke her, and she doesn't have the time Rhyson had to prepare. Emotion soaks her eyes, and a wide smile comes to life on her lips.

"Rhyson," she whispers, none of the irritation and hurt I've seen her fight all day evident. "You're here."

"Yeah, I'm here." I wonder if she notices how his laugh catches a little in his throat. "You're here, too."

The seconds stretch into a minute as they stare at each other, taking in the face so like their own, but so completely different.

"You look . . ." Rhyson tilts his head, studying his sister with sober eyes. "You're beautiful, Bris."

Tears flood her eyes, one sneaking over her cheek. She swipes it away quickly.

"Stop." She smiles self-consciously. "I look the same."

Rhyson shakes his head, brushing her tousled hair back with one hand. "My little sister grew up."

"Little sister?" She quirks one dark brow, some of the spark I saw today returning to her eyes. "We're twins, doofus."

"I was born first," he counters, his crooked smile telling me he's enjoying this.

"And that one minute more in the world gives you so much of an edge?" she fires back.

"Whether you want to admit it or not, you're my little sister." The look he gives her already apologizes before his words do. "I'm sorry we missed the last five years."

"Me, too," she says, the smile dying from her eyes.

"And for missing today. I wish I could say tomorrow would be much different. I have to be in the studio a lot, but you can come with me."

"Okay. That sounds fun." She stretches, yawns, and tosses the blanket off, standing to her feet. "We can talk about it in the morning. I'm off to bed."

"Me, too." Rhyson stands, talking through a yawn. "Marlon, it's so late, you should just crash here tonight."

Bristol's eyes shift over his shoulder, widening like she just realized that I was still here. She offers me a smile more reserved than the ones we exchanged while we talked all night. When we made each other laugh.

"Thanks again, Grip, for keeping me company today."

"No problem." I take the spot and the blanket on the couch she just vacated, not looking up to meet her eyes. "Any time."

I feel her eyes on me. After all we discussed today, all we shared, my tone probably seems impersonal. She may not know it now, but she'll realize soon, that's for her own good. She's something rare—smart, classy, gorgeous, funny, opinionated, and under it all, where she tries to hide it, kind. And burrowed beneath all of that, vulnerable. She isn't the kind of girl you mess over.

I repeat that warning to myself for the next hour as I stare into the darkness of Grady's living room. No, she isn't the kind of girl you mess over. A guy needs to be very sure he wants her, and just her, before he makes a move.

Yeah. A guy would have to be very sure.

7

BRISTOL

"HMMMMM."

I moan as soon as the warm bite of syrup-soaked waffle hits my tongue. "Don't tell me you're a short-order cook, too, when you're not deejaying or sweeping floors or writing songs."

Grip laughs, not looking up from the waffle maker on the kitchen counter. Powder sprinkles his face, right above the corner of his mouth, sugary white against the caramel of his skin. I want to lick it away. That realization has me choking on my waffle.

"You okay?" Rhyson pounds my back like I'm a little girl.

"Yeah." Eyes still watering, I sip my orange juice. "Just went down the wrong way."

Grip brings another stack of waffles to the table.

"Send these down the right way," he says.

Our eyes catch and hold across the table. Sunlight floods Grady's well-appointed kitchen, and you'd never know Grip slept on the couch and hasn't showered. Damn, the man looks good in this light. He'd probably look good in no light. A thin layer of stubble coats his chiseled jaw, and I wouldn't mind rubbing up against it, feeling the scrape as he leaves a mark on me.

My vagina needs a serious pep talk.

"So what's the plan for today?" Grip slices into his stack of waffles.

"Well, I'm in the studio pretty much all day again." He glances at me while he chews. "Sorry about that. It's bad timing but unavoidable."

"It's fine." I pause with my orange juice halfway to my mouth. "You did say I could tag along, right?"

"Won't you be bored?" Rhyson spears a waffle square. "I mean, if you want to come, you can."

"And the alternative would be . . .what?" I ask. "Sitting here in Grady's empty house all day?"

I could make the uncomfortable expression on his face go away, but I won't. I want him to feel the discomfort. I'm spending my spring freaking break here so we can reconnect, and that's what I want us to do.

"You have to be in the studio tonight?" Grip asks.

"Yeah. The singer's coming in to lay some new vocals." Rhyson scowls. "I hope we can knock everything out tonight. Maybe go to Santa Monica Pier tomorrow. But there may be another short session or two."

"If you want, I can swing by the studio to get Bristol tonight on my way to Brew." Grip directs the comment to Rhyson, not looking at me. "Take her with me."

He's barely spoken to me all morning. We talked last night for hours, and if I hadn't conked out, we probably would have talked for hours more. Maybe he has this kind of connection all the time, authentic and easy. He probably stays up all night talking to girls all the time. To me, though, it feels exceptional to be able to talk with someone so openly in such a short time.

"That cool with you, Bris?" Rhyson asks.

"Sure." I check Grip's face for any sign that this is a pain in his ass. "If you don't mind. Aren't you working?"

"Just deejaying." He taps his fork against his lips. "Jimmi will be there, too. You guys can hang."

I chuckle and drag my fork through the sticky syrup on my plate. "She seems cool," I say. "And really talented. She blew the roof off Mick's yesterday."

"They finally let her on stage?" Rhyson rubs his eyes and yawns. "Good for her."

I read between the lines of fatigue on my brother's handsome face.

"You still seem sleepy, Rhys. Why don't you go catch some z's until you have to be at the studio?"

"You sure?" Rhyson's eyes already seem to be drooping at the prospect of crawling back into bed. "I only need like another hour or two, then we can roll out."

"No problem." I walk my plate over to the sink and rinse it off. "I can clean up in here."

"You don't have to clean up after me." A small frown lands between Grip's eyebrows.

"You didn't have to cook for us," I come back, loading my plate and utensils into the dishwasher. "But you did. It was delicious, by the way."

"Glad you enjoyed it," he says politely before looking away. I'm struck again by the contrast from last night when he was warm and open. This morning, he isn't so much cold as he is indifferent. I just met him yesterday and refuse to allow myself a sense of loss. I mean, come on. We had a few intelligent conversations and a couple meals. No big deal.

Keep telling yourself that.

"Take a change of clothes with you to the studio," Grip says. "You can get dressed there before we go to the club."

He comes to the sink, handing me his empty plate. When I tug, he doesn't let go, and we have a childish tug-of-war for a second between our hands and between our eyes. He finally relents, grinning and walking back to the table. Rhyson watches the byplay between Grip and me with eyes that are suddenly alert and speculative.

"I better get going." Grip grabs his backpack from the floor near his seat. "Stuff to do and people to see."

"Thanks again for everything," Rhyson says.

"It's nothing." Grip gives me a smile before waving at us both and disappearing through the kitchen door.

"You know not to get all giddy over Marlon, right?" Rhyson watches me with big brother eyes. "I mean, he's a great guy. My best friend, in fact, but he goes through girls like toilet paper."

"You mean he wipes his ass with them?" I ask with false innocence.

"Good one." Rhyson doesn't grin as he comes to stand beside me at the sink. "Seriously, Bris, all the girls fall for Marlon, and he isn't ready to be good to any one girl."

"And are you?" I challenge him with a smirk, disguising the pinch in my chest hearing him describe Grip. I should be glad he's telling me, though I don't need him warning me about his best friend. "Ready to be good to one girl?"

"Hell, no." Rhyson laughs, crossing his arms over his wide chest. "I want to be as good to as many girls as I can."

We laugh, but once the joke is over, I realize we're alone for the first time since I arrived in LA. Alone for the first time in years. This is nothing like the comfortable silences Grip and I shared yesterday. This is awkward, filled with the memories of the last time we saw each other. We were in a courtroom, and he'd just been awarded his "freedom" from our family. And, boy, did he take flight. He never looked back from that day forward. If I hadn't reached out, there's no telling when we would have reconnected. Maybe never. Maybe he would have been fine with that.

"So how are the folks?" There's a studied relaxation to Rhyson. I may not have seen him in years, but I still recognize the tension in his shoulders. The stiffness of his back belying his false ease. He isn't just waiting for news of our parents. He's braced for it.

"They're good." I load the last plate into the dishwasher. "They talk about you a lot. I know they miss you."

"Miss me? Or the money?" he asks bitterly. "Are they not getting their monthly royalty checks?"

"That isn't fair, Rhyson. I know they didn't handle everything the right way all the time when they managed your career."

"Is that what you call enabling my addiction to prescription drugs so I could get through shows? So they could build their fortune at my expense?" Anger flares in Rhyson's eyes and colors his face. "Spare me the song and dance about them missing me. They have fifty percent of every dime I've ever earned. That was the price they named to let me leave. They aren't getting anything else from me."

I'm quiet for a moment, wondering how much I can press on this wound before he lashes out at me even more.

"And me?" I blink at the tears blurring the vision of my brother in front of me. "Do I get anything else?"

"I didn't know you wanted anything in the settlement, Bristol." Rhyson frowns. "But we can arrange—"

"How dare you?" Indignation tremors through me and makes my voice shake. "I call you. I write you. I text you. I fly to freaking Los Angeles and am hauled around the city all day while you Liberace in the studio, and you have the nerve to think I want your money? I don't need your money, Rhyson. I have a trust fund that will take care of me for the rest of my life if I don't want to work, which I do."

His eyes lay so heavily on me I feel them like a weight. He never looks away from my face when he asks his next question, as if he might catch me in a lie.

"Then why are you here, Bristol? What do you want?"

God, I come here with my heart bleeding on my sleeve, and it's still not enough for him. He needs me to cut it out and hand it to him in chunks of flesh and blood.

"I thought it would be obvious what I want." I tip my chin up defiantly and meet the skepticism and mistrust in his eyes. "I want my brother."

8

BRISTOL

WHEN RHYSON SAID I could come and watch him in the studio, he wasn't lying. That's about all I've gotten to do. He certainly hasn't talked to me much, and I can't imagine the complete focus it takes to create music at this level. Rhyson hasn't budged in eight hours. He's obsessing over four or five notes that, to his ear at least, are not "falling right." Whatever that means. He's barely looked up except when I brought him a sandwich, which still sits half-eaten on the piano.

At least I've knocked out my internship application. Machiavelli is all done.

An irrepressible grin springs to my lips as I remember Grip's reaction to my thinking his tattoo was misspelled. Mental images of the muscled terrain the tattoo adorns melt my grin. I've had plenty of time to remember how much I enjoyed hanging out with him yesterday. Rhyson's warning wasn't necessary, but it remains fresh in my mind.

He isn't ready to be good to any one girl.

And I am but one girl.

I glance down at the cleavage on display in the dress I changed into. Definitely a girl and definitely ready to let off some steam. The painted-on black bandage dress shows off all my assets, especially the ones up top. It lovingly traces the curves of my waist, hips, and ass, leaving my legs bare from mid-thigh. I've left my hair hanging down my back in loose waves. My makeup is smoky eyes and red lips.

"I deserve a night out," I tell the girl in the mirror. "Three thousand miles and I'm closeted in a studio all day?"

The girl in the mirror mocks me with her smoky eyes. She knows as well as I do that I wouldn't have traded today for anything. It felt like old times. Rhyson may have forgotten, but I used to do my homework outside his rehearsal room. I loved hearing my brother play, replaying a passage until it was perfect. That hasn't changed. I may not make music, but I love it. My parents may manage musicians now, but they were both brilliant musicians when they were younger. Uncle Grady, too. I told Grip I was an ugly duckling in my family. Maybe I'm not ugly, but I'm certainly the odd man out.

My eyes drop to the shadowy cleft between my breasts. Correction. Odd woman out.

I slip back into the studio unnoticed, and my heart skips a stupid beat when I see Grip at the piano with Rhyson. Both of their faces, which are so different but so handsome, wear matching frowns of concentration.

"Did you try it here?" Grip points to a place on the pad Rhyson has been scribbling on all day.

"Yeah." Rhyson chews on the end of his pencil. "But it's a major third."

"Ahhhh." Grip nods since that apparently holds significance to him that I don't grasp. "I see."

Neither of them looks up when I step farther into the room, keeping their eyes trained on the pad.

"Oh!" Grip's face lights up. He grabs Rhyson's pencil and music pad, writing furiously, a wide smile spreading over his face. "What about that?"

Rhyson takes the pad, frowning for a few silent moments before laughing and slapping Grip on the back.

"That does it." Rhyson's shoulders slump with his relief. "Man, thanks. I've been looking at it too long. I didn't even see what was right in front of me."

"Glad I could help." Grip's expression shifts, amusement twitching his lips. "Hey, did that guy send you his demo or mixtape or whatever? The guy from Grady's class?"

"That dude." Rhyson grimaces and then shifts into an odd British accent. "I was gonna listen to that, but then I just carried on living my life."

Huh?

"That's one of your goofy ass movie quotes, isn't it?" Grip shakes his head, his grin teasing Rhyson. "Which one?"

"Russel Brand in *Forgetting Sarah Marshall*. You'd like that one."

"That's what you said about *Little Nicky*."

"Okay." Chagrin wrinkles Rhyson's expression. "Upon further consideration, that was an Adam Sandler miss, I admit."

"I've never known anyone as obsessed with movies as you. You got a quote for every day of the week."

Really? I don't remember Rhyson ever watching movies. He never had time. It strikes me—again—how little I know this version of my twin brother. Grady, Grip, and Jimmi seem to all know more about him than I do. Maybe because they're his family now.

"Yeah. You know that's how I decompress." Rhyson returns his attention to the music pad, halfway gone already.

"I can think of several ways to decompress that . . ."

Whatever Grip planned to say goes unsaid when he catches sight of me. His eyes scroll over my body in a quick assessment and then go back up and down for slow seconds. When he finally reaches my face, his eyes burn into mine. His mouth falls open just the tiniest bit, and in that small space between his full lips, I see his tongue dart out for a quick swipe. Like he wants a taste of something. Like he wants a taste of me. It's a nanosecond, but it's real, and I see it before he stashes it away and schools his face into the indifference he showed me in the kitchen this morning.

"Bris, wow." Rhyson's brows disappear under his messy fall of dark hair. "You look . . .wow. Grip, you'll have to protect my little sister at the club tonight."

I saunter closer, my Louboutins adding another inch or so to my confidence and some sway to my hips.

"Maybe I don't want to be protected." I laugh at the nauseous look on Rhyson's face. "This is my spring break, brother, and I am all grown up. I've been in this studio all day working on my essay. I'm ready to be hair down, bottles up, and I'm glad you won't be there cramping my style."

"You finished?" Grip asks, speaking for the first time. "The application?"

"Yeah." We stare at one another for a few seconds before I untangle our eyes. The leftover heat in his gaze is still too hot for me. "I'll read over the essay one more time before I submit."

"What's this essay for anyway?" Rhyson asks from behind the piano, linking his hands behind his head.

"An internship I'm applying for with Sound Management." I watch his face to see if it sinks in for him.

"Sound Management?" Rhyson bunches his brows. "They manage some huge acts. What's your major?"

"Business. But my emphasis will be entertainment. Entertainment management is what I want to do."

I feel Grip's eyes on me. I hadn't mentioned that in all our discussions about music yesterday. I wanted to talk with Rhyson about this myself.

"Following in our parents' footsteps." Cynicism twists Rhyson's lips. "Shocking."

"Well, it is the family business." I shrug my shoulders nonchalantly. "Besides, maybe you'll need someone you can trust to manage you when the time comes. I want to learn everything I can. Maybe move here after graduation."

Two sets of eyes snap to my face, Rhyson's and Grip's. Even pointedly eyeing my manicure, I feel them both looking at me.

"What the hell?" Rhyson's face is somewhere between thunder-struck and thundercloud, shock and anger competing. "Manage me doing what? I'm not a performer anymore, Bristol, and I won't be."

I give up feigning interest in my nails and focus all my will on my brother, even managing to block out Grip's magnetic presence.

"You are a genius, Rhyson." I set my face in stone. "One of the most brilliant pianists to ever live. There is no way you're supposed to spend the rest of your life writing music for other people and producing their stuff."

"Did Mother put you up to this?" Rhyson levels a cold stare at me. "I knew it. You come here all 'I want my brother back', but this is your agenda. Their agenda. To get me under their control again."

"Fuck you, Rhyson." The words erupt from the pool of lava boiling in my belly. "I'm the one who has made any effort to maintain a relationship between us, not you."

"Yeah, and I know why." His anger, which matches mine, slams into me. "They couldn't get me back themselves, so they use you to manipulate me."

"Use me?" A bark of laughter hurts my throat. "Why would they ever think I had any influence over you? When have you ever cared about me, Rhyson? If they didn't know by the absolute disregard you had for me when you lived at home, surely they would have known by the way you cut me out of your life when you left."

The anger on his face stutters, going in and out like a bulb with a short.

"Wait. Known what?" Bewilderment puckers his expression. "What would they know, Bristol?"

"That you haven't ever given a damn about me." Emotion over-takes me, inundating my throat, burning my face, saturating my eyes. "They have to know that. I certainly do."

"That isn't true, Bris." He runs a hand through his hair, his move-ments jerky. "Look, this escalated fast. I shouldn't have—"

"No, you shouldn't have."

Someone entering the studio silences us both, curtailing our argument. A guy around our age wearing headphones looped around his neck pauses, watching the three of us cautiously.

"Sorry." He adjusts his black-rimmed glasses. "Rhys, am I early or …"

"No. We, um . . .I'm ready." Rhyson propels a sigh, looking at me.

"Bristol, I—"

"Are we going to this club or what?" I cut him off, slicing a look Grip's way.

"Uh . . ." Grip's eyes skid from me to my brother. "Maybe you should—"

"Never mind. I'll go by myself."

I charge down the hall, my red bottoms making a meal of the carpet and eating up inches with every step. I'm almost at the studio exit by the time Grip catches me, grabbing my elbow and turning me to face him.

"You don't even know where you're going, Bristol." Concern and irritation blend in his eyes.

"I'm pretty good at figuring shit out." I tug on my arm. "Let go."

"Just calm the hell down." He scowls and doesn't let me go. "Come on. The car's parked out front."

I follow him to his Jeep, blinking at the tears rising up as I mentally replay the argument with Rhyson. How dare he question my motives? I've gone above and beyond to show him how important he is to me, and he insults me? Doesn't trust me? I'm tempted to demand that Grip stop the car and hitch a ride to the airport. Just leave all my crap at Grady's and go back to New York right now.

"You're both so damn stubborn." Grip negotiates the traffic, sparing me a quick glance.

"Me?" My harsh laugh bounces off the Jeep's interior. "He's the one."

"You know he's just hurt, Bristol."

"He's hurt?" I turn in my seat to face him, the seatbelt cutting into my chest. "He's the one who left five years ago. He's the one who acted like I was a nuisance every time I reached out. And then I come out here on my spring break, just to have him work the whole time. I swear he's using it as an excuse not to deal with me."

"He does have actual work," Grip inserts.

"And he's the one hurt?" I power on. "The hell." "You can't control him, Bristol."

"Contr . . .you're on his side." Even though Rhyson is Grip's best friend and I've only known him a day, I feel betrayed. "You think I'm trying to control my brother? I'm trying to help him fulfill his dreams."

"No, they're not his dreams." Grip shakes his head adamantly, eyes trained ahead. "Not right now. They're your dreams for him. The same way your parents worked him to death doing their dreams. It feels the same to him."

"It isn't the same." I say it even though what he says makes sense. I don't want to accept it. He takes my pause as the chance to speak some more.

"Think about it." Grip's voice gentles, and the look he sends me from behind the wheel gentles, too. "Their priorities weren't straight. They seemed more concerned with the career than with him. When you take the reins like you did back there, it makes him think that you're just like them, especially your mom."

I let that set in for a second, let it sink through my pores and trickle down to my heart. It hurts because, though I love my mother and have done all I could to please her, she's a hard-nosed bitch.

Am I?

"You're not like her," Grip says softly, as if he read my mind. "At least not the way he described her to me. You're not that."

I turn my head and look out the window so he won't see my lip trembling or the tears quivering on my lashes. It feels like I keep hiding from him when he seems to see everything.

"Maybe I am," I whisper. "I just . . .he's so talented. I will never believe he's supposed to be some hack who just writes for other people."

I whip my head around, eyes wide. "No offense."

"None taken." Grip laughs, the cocky smirk firmly in place. "I already know I got the goods. It's just a matter of time and the right opportunity before I'm on somebody's stage."

His smirk disappears when he glances at me.

"For me and for Rhyson. I actually am on your side in this. I believe he should be doing his own music, too, and he will. But he has to come to it for himself."

I bite my thumbnail and shake my head, turning my eyes back to the traffic crawling by.

"How do you guys live with this traffic?" I ask, needing to dispel some of the heaviness in the car.

"Like New York's much better?"

"True. But you don't have to drive in New York."

"Well, it sounds like you may have to endure it with the rest of us soon." We're sitting still, jammed in a tight line of vehicles, so he looks at me fully, a question in his eyes before he asks it. "Were you serious about moving here when you graduate?"

I nod and swallow my nerves as I wonder if he's asking for Rhyson or if he might have a personal interest in my relocating to the West Coast.

"That's the plan." A self-deprecating smile wrings my lips. "The ridiculous plan based on Rhyson doing something he has no intention of doing. You must think I'm crazy, huh?"

"It is crazy."

My heartbeat stumbles. I know it's farfetched. I know it's irrational to stake my entire college career, my future, on the dreams Rhyson isn't even dreaming, but to hear Grip affirm my lunacy chafes. Then his lips, which are a contradiction of soft and sculpted, curve into something especially for me. A smile just for me. When he turns to look at me, it warms his dark eyes.

"And I don't know what Rhyson did to deserve you," he says.

9

BRISTOL

I'M NOT SURE I like this club.

Another scantily dressed woman walks over to the booth and passes Grip a slip of paper, presumably with her number on it.

That might have something to do with why I don't like this club. And it's ridiculous. I met the man yesterday. But in my defense,

we've squeezed weeks of conversation into the last two days. Still, that doesn't excuse the jealousy gnawing my insides. When I add that to the lingering hurt from my argument with Rhyson, it makes it impossible for me to enjoy myself.

"Are we gonna dance or just hold up the bar all night?" Jimmi moves her shoulders and ass to the Drake song in Grip's rotation.

"Sorry. I'm not a very good dancer." I shrug, not really sorry. "And I'm kind of tired."

And horny.

My midterms took it out of me. The internship essay took it out of me. This trip has taken it out of me. I need a good drink and a good lay, in that order. I don't know Jimmi well enough to confess it. She'd probably hook me up with some stranger, and that isn't what I want.

That isn't who I want.

I glance over at the booth where Grip has been all night, keeping the music going.

I'm not letting myself go there. I purposely look away, only to clash eyes with some frat looking guy a few feet away eye fucking me. He flashes me a too-white smile. That smile would glow in the dark. I don't return it, but deliberately look away, hoping he gets the message.

The message being no.

"I love this song," Jimmi says. "Grip has great mixes."

"Yeah, he does." I sip my Grey Goose, waiting for the buzz that will numb the hurt Rhyson inflicted. Something to take the edge off this sexy itch I haven't scratched in months.

Months?

Well, damn. No wonder I'm horny.

"So what do you think of him?" Jimmi asks. I obviously missed something.

"Huh? Sorry." I set my hurt feelings and needy libido aside long enough to focus on Jimmi's pretty face. "Who? What do I think of who?"

"Grip." Jimmi sneaks me a curious glance. "All girls have thoughts about Grip when they first meet him."

"Um . . .he's nice?" I set my drink down and turn my stool to face the wall of bottles behind the bar. "He's my brother's best friend. That about sums it up."

"Oh, the two of them together." Jimmi fans herself. "They've been double trouble since high school."

She touches my arm, her eyes contrite.

"I'm sorry. That's your brother I'm talking about. Awkward." She gives my hand a reassuring pat. "Rhyson's nowhere near as bad as Grip, though."

"As bad?" I swirl the contents of my glass without looking at her. "What do you mean?"

"Oh, Grip goes through girls like it's nothing." Jimmi lets out a husky laugh. "They're disposable."

"I can imagine," I answer weakly. She's only echoing what Rhyson already told me. The guy I talked to for hours yesterday doesn't match the one they're describing, but they know him better than I do. "But I heard he makes it worth their while." Jimmi wiggles her eyebrows suggestively. "One of my girls got with him. She says he's hung like you wouldn't believe."

Not what my vagina needs to hear right now. I cross my legs and squirm in my seat, seeking some friction, some release. The alcohol is kicking in, and it only fires the need in me. I imagine all those inches stretching me and ... I need to rub up against something.

"Are you not into Black guys?" Jimmi scrunches her nose. "I mean, I have some friends who aren't. I don't care. I'd screw a hole in the wall if it could make me come."

"Wow. That's a . . .colorful way to say it. No, I've never dated a Black guy, but I guess I just never had the opportunity." I shrug. "I don't really care."

Especially if he looked like Grip. I'd take green Grip. Pink Grip. Red Grip. If Grip were a bag of Skittles, I'd eat every one.

"Oh." Jimmi claps excitedly. "Grip's gonna perform."

"He is?" I perk up, spinning around on my stool. Sure enough, he's on stage with a mic. Under the lights, he seems even taller, even broader.

"What's good?" Grip spreads his smile around the club. "I don't get to do this as much as I'd like, but they're gonna let me spit a few bars for you tonight."

The cheering and whistles and catcalls explode from the audience.

"I see my reputation precedes me." Grip chuckles and nods to the drummer in the corner. "Lil' somethin' for you."

I wasn't lying when I told Grip I don't listen to rap much. I don't hate it. I've just always been indifferent. I can't make out half of what they're saying, and once I know, it's all bitches and hos and slurs. I wince through half of it and roll my eyes through the rest. It's just not my favorite music. But Grip is a different breed. I understand every word he says, and I'm hanging on every one. Literally waiting for the next syllable. The images he paints are so vivid that, if I closed my eyes, they'd be spray painted on the back of my eyelids. I'd be drowning in color, floating in sound. The richness of his voice floods the room, and I realize he has us all rapt. We're eating his words, a feeding frenzy of imagination. He's a storyteller and a poet.

I feel the same as I did listening to Rhyson growing up. Like the sun and the moon were in my house. Like I was a part of Rhyson's great galaxy, and he was the star. Grip is a star. Sweeping floors and doing all the things he does to survive are all just dues he's paying. He's lightning in a beautiful bottle, just waiting to strike. A pending storm. He's hypnotizing. Intoxicating. I'm as buzzed off him as I am off my Grey Goose.

"He's good, right?" Jimmi grins at me knowingly. "I felt the same way the first time I heard him. It's his writing. His stuff is so much deeper than most of what's out there. He's really saying something."

"Yeah." I clear my throat and try to appear less mesmerized. "He's really good. Wow."

"Don't look now, but we aren't the only ones who think so." She nudges me with her elbow and inclines her head toward a group of girls clustering around Grip. "Did you ride with Grip?"

"Uh, yeah." I can't force my eyes away from where he sits on the edge of the stage, girls buzzing around him. He did say you catch more bees with honey.

Or, in his case, chocolate.

"I may be taking you home," she says with a slight smile. "Those are what I like to call 'ground floor groupies'. They see his potential same as we do, and some of them want in on the action before the rest of the world gets a taste of him."

My muscles lock up as I watch several girls stroke his arms and press against his side. That he doesn't see through it makes me sick, souring my high after his performance.

"I think I do want to dance." I knock back my drink and turn to find frat guy, who's still a few feet away. "With him."

I point him out, and before Jimmi can ask me any questions or try to stop me, I'm gone. I walk up to glow-bright smile, and enjoy seeing his eyes get wider the closer I get. Yep. He's one of those. All bold and staring with no idea what to do with it.

"Hey." I step so close I smell the whiskey on his breath. "You've been staring at me all night."

"Uh, you're hot," he stammers, his eyes rolling over my body and sticking to my breasts.

Has it come to this?

"So . . .you want to dance?" I prompt. I'm not a great dancer, but the alcohol humming through my blood convinces me that I am.

"Sure."

I walk onto the dance floor, assuming he's following. Assuming he's staring at my ass as I pop my hips in a loose-limbed sway. His hands clamp my waist, his fingers drifting down to spread over the curves of my butt. I press my back to his chest and start moving, start reaching for a feeling, any feeling to block the emotions that have ravaged me over the last few hours. The hurt and jealousy. The disappointment and resentment. He gets stiffer and harder with every measure of the song, with every roll of my hips. He pulls my hair aside, and his breath lands heavy and hot on my neck. Whatever my body is reaching for, I'm not finding it with him. I'm about to pull away and go order another Grey Goose, when I hear a deep voice behind me.

"Dude, step off."

Gravel studs Grip's voice. Whether he's irritated with me or glow-bright, I don't know. I whirl around to face them. My partner, apparently more a lover than a fighter, has obliged Grip's request and is already halfway back to his frat boy friends.

"What the hell do you think you're doing?" I demand.

"I was just about to ask you the same thing." The club lights stripe his handsome face, painting him in shades of pink and blue and green. "You were working that guy up for nothing."

"For nothing?" I raise both brows, hands on my hips. "It wouldn't have been for nothing. Have you forgotten? This is my spring break.

Girls get drunk and they get laid. I'm already halfway to one, and you just ruined the other."

His face goes hard as cement.

"You're still hurt from your fight with Rhyson." He shakes his head. "I'm not letting you go home with anyone half-drunk and emotional."

"I wasn't going home with him. I would have fucked him in a bathroom stall. In the alley. We would have figured it out."

The light strobes the emotions on his face, flashing anger then frustration.

"I'm gonna excuse that because I know you're upset." "I'm not upset," I snap. "I'm horny."

"Shit, Bristol." He glances at the people dancing within earshot. "That is not what you say in a club full of frat boys trolling for ass. I'm trying to protect you from all these dicks."

"I like dick!" I say a little too loudly, drawing a few more stares. Boy, that Grey Goose has kicked in after all. "And you're cock blocking."

"Cock block . . ." Grip's mouth drops open then snaps shut. "Let's go. You're exhausted and irrational, so Imma give you a pass."

"I'm not going anywhere with you."

I slip past him and stomp off the floor as much as my Louboutins will allow. I have no idea how we got into the club, and I make several turns and detours. I'm sure I'm headed toward the entrance, but I end up behind the building instead of in front. I step out anyway, hauling in a cleansing breath and leaning against the brick wall to calm the tremors shivering through my body. Grinding into glow-bright did nothing for me, but catching a whiff of Grip's clean masculine scent, feeling the warmth of his body as he stood so close—that has me trembling.

"I told Jimmi we'll see her later." Grip walks toward me in the alleyway. "Let's get you home."

My anger has died off, and so has his, apparently. His voice is gentle, his eyes compassionate. He sees too clearly, too much. He detects all the hurt festering under my clingy bandage dress. I hate that he's so sweet and still a player. I won't forget about the bees. And the honey. And the chocolate.

"God, just leave me alone." Pressing into the brick wall at my back, I hold my head in my hands. "I've already told you I'm horny, and you just keep . . ."

I growl and fist my hair and my frustration in my fingers. "You're right." I stand straight. "Let's just go."

I push off the wall at my back only to collide with a wall of muscles and heat at my front. Neither of us makes a move to put any distance between us. My breath stutters over my lips as I fight the magnetic pull of him. We stand there in the alley, trapped in a sensual stasis, unmoving except for our chests heaving against each other's with each labored breath. His hands find the curve of my waist, the dip of my back. He doesn't press me to him, but his touch scorches through the thin material of my dress. He drops his head, pressing his temple to mine, and draws in a breath behind my ear.

"Did you just . . ." I search for the right word, "whiff me?"

His husky laugh leaves warm breath at my neck, skittering a shiver down my spine.

"It's better than the alternative," he says.

"Which is what?" I pull back to peer up at his face.

"Kissing you." His eyes boil from caramel to hot chocolate. Sweet, hot, steamy need spikes in the look he pours over me.

"I'm not doing this with you, Grip." I close my eyes, my hands covering his on my hips. I mean to push them away, but my fingers won't move. They trap his touch against me.

"We just met yesterday," I remind him and myself.

"I know." He shakes his head. "You're my best friend's sister."

"I live in New York."

"I'm here in LA."

"I don't even know you." I laugh a little. "And what I do know is not good. You're a player."

"Who told you that?" Irritation crinkles his expression.

"Um, you basically did." I roll my eyes. "And Jimmi. And Rhyson."

"They shouldn't . . ." He sighs, releasing his frustration into the stale alley air. "I understand why they would say that, but this isn't . . . you're not . . ."

He bites his bottom lip, a gesture that seems so uncertain when he's been anything but.

"Don't be upset with them for telling me the obvious," I say. "I saw all those girls tonight for myself. I know what it's like for musicians."

"I don't even know those girls."

"You barely know me, either."

He doesn't reply, but the way he looks at me—the pull between us —defies my statement. We know each other. Not in terms of hours or days, but something deeper. Something more elemental, I can't deny it, but I have no idea what to do with it.

"Look, I can admit I'm attracted to you." Grip surveys my body one more time before clenching his eyes closed and giving his head a quick shake. "Damn, that dress, Bristol. All fucking night."

An involuntary smile tugs at my lips, but I pinch it into a tiny quirk of the lips instead of the wide, satisfied thing sprawling inside me.

"Not all night." I firm my lips. "You had quite the fan base. Women lined up after your performance."

"Thirsty chicks." Grip grimaces. "Banking on the off chance that one day I'll be something they can eat off of. Maybe get themselves a baby daddy. Get some bills paid every month."

"It isn't an off chance," I say softly. "It's a certainty."

"What's a certainty?" A frown conveys his confusion.

"That you'll be something one day." I point toward the door leading back into the club. "When you grabbed that mic, when you took that stage, it was obvious you're as talented as Rhyson. It looks and sounds different, but you both have that special quality that makes people watch and listen. You can't teach that or train it. You either have it or you don't."

I offer a smile.

"And you have it."

Surprise and then something else, maybe self-consciousness, cross his face. For one so bold and sure, it's funny to see.

"Yeah, well, thanks." He shrugs and goes on. "Anyway, I know the deal. My mama schooled me on girls like that."

"Your mother sounds very wise."

"Very. She made sure I knew their game."

He waves a hand between our chests.

"This, what we're feeling," he says, his eyes going sober. "It isn't a game."

I hold my breath, waiting for him to tell me we should jump off this cliff. That as crazy as it seems, we'll hold on tight and break each other's fall.

"It's complicated." He lowers his eyes before lifting them to meet mine. "It's just an attraction, and we should probably resist it. I mean, you're only here a few days. If things didn't work out for us, it could make shit awkward with Rhyson, and I know you want to repair things with him. There's a million reasons we shouldn't act on this attraction. Right?"

"Right." I offer a decisive nod. "A million reasons."

As we ride back to Grady's bungalow in our first strained silence since we met at the airport, I realize he was wise to stop whatever could have happened in the alley. It would probably have been a half-drunken regret. There are a million reasons we should stop. But right now, I can only think of the one reason not to stop.

Because I don't want to.

10

BRISTOL

THE RIDE HOME from Brew is mostly silent. Yet, it's a silence filled with all the reasons Grip and I shouldn't indulge the attraction plaguing us. Grip's scent alone—more than clean, less than cologne, and somehow uniquely his—makes me close my eyes and take it in with sneaky sniffs. I wonder if he's taking me in, too. I still tingle from that alleyway alchemy, the chemistry that snapped and sizzled between us behind the club. It's all I can think of.

"We're here." His voice is deep and low in the confines of the car.

I glance at Grady's house, which is dark except for the porch light, and wonder if Rhyson is home, awake, interested in finishing the argument we started earlier. Because who doesn't want to scratch and claw with their sister at two o'clock in the morning?

"Thanks." I turn a grateful smile on him, not meeting his eyes. I fumble with the handle until the door opens, the cool air raising goose bumps on my arms. Or maybe that's his touch, the gentle hand at my elbow. I look back to him, waiting for whatever he has to say.

"Bristol, I . . ." He bunches his brow and gives a quick shake of his head before turning to face forward. Both hands on the wheel of the ancient Jeep. "Never mind."

"Um, okay." I get out, ready to slam the door when his words stop me again.

"I had fun tonight." He leans across the middle console so I can see his face a little. His interior light doesn't work, so he's still basically in the dark. The shadows smudge the striking details of his face, but I feel the intensity of his eyes.

"You had fun wrangling a half-drunk girl off the dance floor and arguing in a dirty alleyway?" I ask sarcastically. "Yeah, right."

I hear the little huff of a laugh from the driver's seat.

"I had fun hanging with you," he responds softly, the smile tinting his voice. I let his words settle over me for a moment before I pat the roof of the car twice and step back.

"Me, too," I finally answer. "Have a good night and thanks for everything."

Manners.

As Grip pulls away from the curb, I can't help but wonder why I'm being painfully polite when what I'm starting to feel for him is anything but well mannered.

A little wild. A lot unexpected. Completely unlikely, but definitely not polite.

I use the key Rhyson gave me and hope there isn't an alarm. I walk deeper into the house, still a little wired but unsure what to do. The door leading to the kitchen opens, and Rhyson steps into the living room.

"Hey," I say softly, watching for signs of lingering anger.

"Hey." His eyes fix on my face, and I'm guessing he's gauging me, too. "You too tired to talk?"

I sit on the couch and gesture for him to join me. He sits, elbows to his knees and eyes on the floor.

"I'm sorry for how out of control things got at the studio," he says, his voice quiet, subdued. "I . . .I don't feel like we know each other anymore."

A humorless laugh escapes my lips.

"And I'm not sure we ever did." I smile a little sadly when our eyes connect around that truth in the lamplight.

"You're probably right."

He sighs, raking his long sensitive fingers through wild hair. He has an artist's hands. Well kempt but competent and capable of creating.

"Do you remember when they insured your hands?" I ask.

"Yeah." He doesn't say anything more, but draws his brows draw into a frown.

"I overheard Mother discussing the policy. We were eleven." I bite my lip and smile. "I remember asking her why they insured your hands. She said you insure things that are too valuable to lose forever. She said your gift was irreplaceable and that made you incredibly valuable. They had to protect you."

"That sounds about right," Rhyson says bitterly. "Protect their investment."

I don't acknowledge his interpretation of it because he never saw it from my side.

"I was so jealous of you that day." I shake my head, feeling that helplessness and the frustration of having nothing to offer flood me again. "I had nothing to insure. I had nothing that valuable to our parents. They had shown me a million times, but that day she put it in words."

"Jealous?" Rhyson's incredulity twists his handsome face. "You were jealous of me? You had everything, Bristol. You had friends. You got to go to school with kids our age. You had a normal life. That was all I wanted."

"You had them," I counter. "The three of you would go off for weeks at a time, and I had nannies and therapists. You had our parents."

"I had them?" Rhyson demands in rhetorical disbelief. "Yeah, I had them riding my ass to rehearse eight hours a day, reminding me that I might be a kid, but adults paid good money to come see me play. I had nothing."

"You loved piano," I insist, needing to know that things are as I remember them, because if they aren't, what has been real?

"I loved piano, yes, but that just came to me. I don't even remember not knowing how to play. Piano I was born with. The career? The road and the concerts and the tours? That they made me do."

Condemnation colors his eyes.

"The addiction—I let that happen," he says.

"You were too young," I counter softly. "Too young to take the pills, and our parents should have stopped you, not enabled you. I see that now."

He scoots closer, looking at me earnestly.

"Bris, I had to get away from them." He shakes his head, and his eyes are bleak. "To survive. I needed to get better, and to do that, I had to put as much distance between them and myself as possible."

"But that meant me, too." Tears prick my eyes.

"Yeah, I'm sorry about that." He drops his head into his hands. "But you stayed. You were there. I didn't know whose side you were on."

"There wasn't a side, Rhyson." My words come vehemently. "You were all my family. They weren't perfect, far from it, but they were the only parents I had. I wanted them to love me. You were the only brother I had. The only family I had, and it was ripped apart. You didn't seem to want to repair it."

"Not with them, no," he admits. "Not yet. Maybe not ever." "And me?" My heart flutters in my chest as I wait.

"When you would call, I thought it was them having you check up on me or trying to get in so they could get me back to make money for them. Even when you called and told me you wanted to come here for spring break, I thought there was an ulterior motive."

He laughs, eyeing me with no small amount of doubt.

"And when you started talking today about moving here and managing my career—"

"I probably should have handled that better." It's the truth. "I know it seems crazy to you, but you're a star, Rhyson. Like once-in-a-lifetime genius star. I don't want to capitalize on it. I just want to see it happen, and for some reason, it isn't."

"I don't know if I can do that shit again, Bris. It takes so much, and I only got through it with the drugs. I don't want to create a situation where I need those again. If there was one thing I learned when I kicked the habit, it was that I have an addictive personality. Music is the only thing I need to be addicted to."

"I'm not trying to create a situation where you need the drugs," I say. "I just want to be your sister again."

"And my manager?" Skepticism lifts one of his brows. "You want to be that, too?"

"I still have two years left at Columbia. We could start with me just being your sister." A wide smile stretches across my face at the prospect. "And then see what happens."

11

GRIP

I HATE CARNIVALS.

My cousin Jade used to drag me to these things and make me stay until the smell of funnel cake wasn't even sweet anymore. We'd ride the Ferris wheel and run through the fun house. We'd play every game we could afford and some we managed to swindle our way into. Ring toss. Big Six Wheel. Ring the Bell. Skeeball. Jade's so competitive, I'd have to let her win the basket toss most of the time. Not so much she'd get suspicious, but enough that she didn't pout the whole damn time.

Something shifted between Jade and me along the way. I know it started with a secret shame we share, and over time, that deteriorated our closeness some. When I won the scholarship, leaving her in our local public school, things only worsened. We're still close, but it isn't what it was before. Maybe it's just a part of growing up.

All that to say, I hate carnivals.

And Jimmi's "brill" idea (her whack word, not mine) to show Bristol some fun before she leaves is this carnival. It could be worse.

Rhyson could be stuck in the studio again, and I could be enter-
taining Bristol by myself. And that could get touchy . . .since I want to
fuck her.

I mean, yes, talk to her till the sun comes up, laugh about the
stand-up comedians we both like, exchange playlists, debate hot-
button politics, explore all the ways we are different and just alike . .
.but also I want to fuck her.

And never more so than last night in the alley. That sensuality I
wasn't sure Bristol understood about herself gyrated on the dance
floor. The way her eyes dropped closed when she took her first sip of
Grey Goose, licking the drops from her lips and savoring their taste.
The way she rolled her hips, even sitting on her stool, her body
seeking out the primal beat of the music. She says she can't dance,
but it wasn't skill that had her out on the floor. It was her body
pinned up, searching for release. And she thought she would find it
with that Zeta Delta Dick frat boy who had been scoping her all
night. I could barely focus from song to song as I watched her.
Watched him watching her. I knew I couldn't give her the release she
wanted, but he certainly wasn't going to.

It feels like this has been building between us for months, but it's
only been days. I had decided to squelch it, but when I heard her
master plan about moving to LA and managing Rhyson, something
turned over inside my head. A possibility? A maybe? Doing what
she's doing, staking her college career, planning her future based on
helping her brother's dreams come true, it's crazy.

And so completely right.

I've known since the beginning that Rhyson will have to play
again. We use the word genius like it's nothing. I mean, seriously.
Apple genius? But he is legit genius. Like playing Beethoven at three
years old genius. And for him to neglect his gift, in whatever form it
takes—classical, modern, pop, rock—is a travesty. Everyone around
him knows it. Jimmi, our friend Luke, Grady. I know it, but none of us
have called him on it. We have this silent pact to let him come to it on
his own. He has to after what he endured for years under his parents'
tyrannical management. But Bristol, who hasn't even seen him in five

years, does it. She's so sure it's right that she's betting her Ivy League education on it. She's planning her future around it. She's challenging him in a way none of us were willing to do.

And that's my kind of girl. That abandoned passion. That bottomless commitment. You don't meet people like her often, and when you do, you never forget them. I couldn't get her out of my mind before, but now ...

I glance over at Bristol and Jimmi, who are playing water guns with Rhyson. It's good to see the siblings laughing. Maybe they worked things out after I dropped Bristol off last night. They seem to be trying to enjoy the little time they have left. She leaves in two days. Why that feels so shitty this fast baffles me.

"Come on, Grip!" Jimmi eyes me over her shoulder as she sprays blindly at the target in front of her. "Grab a gun."

"Nah." I munch on the popcorn I grabbed a few booths back. "I'm good."

Carnivals do have good popcorn. But funnel cake? I ate so much of it with Jade, the smell nauseates me. When they finish the game, the girls want to do rides.

"Ferris wheel." Jimmi presses her hands together in a plea to Rhyson. "Please ride with me."

Rhyson carefully considers the girl who has been one of our closest friends since high school. She's also had a crush on Rhyson about as long as she's known him. He's very careful with her heart, though, encouraging her as little as possible. Rhyson gets as much ass as I do, but he's just on the low with his shit. He knows there should be a huge KEEP OUT sign all over him for Jimmi.

"Okay, we can ride." Rhyson holds up an index finger. "Once, Jim. I know how you get. All 'again, again'."

"Cool." Jimmi's expression may be calm, but her eyes dance all over the place. "We can talk about that song I'm working on."

She knows him well. As soon as she says that, Rhyson is in. Talking music theory and asking about chord changes will occupy them for the whole ride.

"We're down to ride, too." Luke, the other guy we've been tight with for years and a fellow arts alum, hooks his elbow around his girlfriend Mandi's neck.

"I ate that Polish sausage." Mandi looks a little green. "Think I'll be okay on the Ferris wheel?"

I wouldn't trust it. You can't ever un-see projectile vomit, and there's nothing sexy about that.

"So, you'll ride with Grip then, Bristol?" Jimmi looks between the two of us with a gleam in her eye. Don't let the blonde hair fool ya. Jimmi's sharp as a new pair of scissors. She probably picked up on the vibe between Bristol and me last night. We don't need her matchmaking. I'm trying to figure out how not to complicate this situation more. The last thing we need is be alone on the—

"I'll ride." Bristol stuffs her hands into her pockets and looks at her feet. "I mean, if you want to, Grip. Since everyone else is. Up to you."

She looks up at me, wearing not much makeup at all. Just as beautiful. A threat to my peace of mind.

"Weren't you scared of heights?" Rhyson asks his sister, a reminiscent smile playing around his lips.

Surprise flits across Bristol's face.

"Uh, yeah. For a little while. Sometimes." She laughs, covering her mouth with one hand. "Mother sent me to therapy for it. Remember that?"

"God, yes." Rhyson's face lights up. "Didn't she send you to therapy for biting your nails, too?"

"And for wetting the bed. I was three! Since she was never there, therapy was Mother's parenting alternative," Bristol says dryly.

Wow. Their mom does sound like a piece of work, but Rhyson and Bristol are laughing about it as if it's nothing that their mother sent a three-year-old to therapy for bed-wetting. Just two prisoners, reminiscing about doing their time. Only Rhyson escaped, and Bristol stayed behind bars.

The ride is crowded, and there aren't any available cars near each other, so we're all spread out, leaving Bristol and me strapped into this small space and relatively alone. At first, the only sound is the whir of the motor and distant squeals from the ground below. After a few moments of quiet between us, Bristol snickers. I glance at her to see what's so funny, but she isn't even looking at me. She's looking down at the ground, which is growing smaller and smaller as we ascend.

"What?" I ask. "You laughed. What's up?"

She turns her head, and her laughter slowly leaks away until the only thing left of it is a shadow in her eyes.

"I was thinking about my mom sending me to therapy for biting my nails." She shakes her head. "I spent so much time in therapy, I knew the therapists about as well as I knew my nannies."

"You had nannies?"

"Sure." She laughs again, but this time bitterness tinges the sound. "Who else was going to raise me with my parents trailing Rhyson on the road most of the year?"

"That sucks."

I want to say more, but feel it might the wrong thing. Like how her mom should have stayed her ass at home with Bristol instead of forcing Rhyson to perform most of his childhood or leaving him addicted to prescription drugs. But that might be too much.

We reach the top of the wheel, and both of us look over our respective sides at the ground. When I turn back into the car, Bristol's face has gone pale, and her breath comes in little anxious puffs.

"Hey, you okay?" I lean into her space, grasping her chin to turn her face to me.

"Yeah. I just—" She closes her eyes and clamps her teeth down on her bottom lip. "I shouldn't have looked down."

"Are you still scared of heights?"

"Sometimes." Her eyes are still closed, and she pulls in deep breaths through her nose and blows them out through her mouth. "This used to help."

"If you're still scared of heights, why'd you want to ride this thing?"

When she opens her eyes, I almost wish she hadn't. There's a vulnerability at odds with Bristol's bold persona. There's a question there that she's afraid to voice, and I know just as surely as if she'd said it aloud that she got on this ride to spend time with me. She drops her lashes and fidgets, bending her body over the bar holding us in and folding her arms on top of it.

"Just don't look down." I clear my throat, looking away from her, too. "We'll be finished soon."

Only we don't move at all for the next few seconds. And then more seconds.

"What's going on?" Low-level panic infiltrates her voice. "Why aren't we moving?"

"They just kind of pause sometimes," I lie. "Probably just so we can get a good look at everything."

Her laugh catches me off guard.

"They just kind of pause?" She rolls her eyes, looking more like the confident Bristol I've gotten to know the last few days. "You're a better liar than that."

"I don't lie." I shrug. "Ask anybody. I'm honest as Abe. You know how you're in a group and someone farts? And no one claims it?"

"Don't tell me." She giggles, resting her cheek on her folded arms and looking at me. "You claim it."

"If I do it, then I claim it." I grin at her, glad to see some of the color returning to her face. "I have no shame, but at least I'm honest about my shit."

Just as I'm thinking crisis averted, an announcement reaches our ears from the ground that there is a technical problem they're working on, and we should be moving in a few minutes.

"Minutes?" Bristol peers back over her side.

"Don't look down, Bris." I've never shortened her name before like that, the way Rhyson does, and I shouldn't like how intimate it feels.

"Okay. I promise not to freak out unless they leave us up here much longer."

"And if we are up here much longer?"

"Then I can't make any promises." She runs an anxious hand through her hair. "I'm not scared of heights in general. I can go up elevators and stuff. This is the only thing left from my old fear. Being in an open ride like this and suspended over the ground. I just can't stop thinking that I could fall so easily."

The more she talks about it, the more the color vacates her cheeks and her breath chops up again.

"Okay, let's distract you until we get moving again." I roam my brain for something to take her mind off the imagined fall to our death. "What's the weirdest place you ever had sex?"

Yep. The girl I'm supposed to be not trying to screw, and that's the question that comes to mind. Live by the dick, die by the dick, I guess. No going back now, so I just wait for her response like it's not a moronic question.

"Um, how do you know I've had sex before?" Her eyes and her grin collaborate to tease me. "Maybe I'm a virgin."

"Weren't you the girl who screamed 'I like dick' at the top of her lungs last night on the dance floor?" I throw my head back and guffaw, in honor of Jimmi and her word-challenged self.

"Oh my God." Pink washes over her high cheekbones. "I can't believe I did that. It was the Grey Goose talking."

"And warned me that you were horny like you might pounce on me if I got too close." My laugh dies down to a smile, even though this conversation is making my jeans tight.

"Okay, you can stop humiliating me now." She's only half-joking but twists her mouth to the side. "Coat check."

"What?" Is the height going to her head already? "What's coat check?"

"That's the weirdest place I ever had sex. It was at my debutante ball, and—"

"You were a debutante?"

"Don't ask. My mother's doing." She sighs and offers a wry smile. "But my date and I snuck into the coat check closet and did it. I had on this huge white dress and he was struggling to find the condom and the heel on my shoe ..."

She waves her hand dismissively and grins. "I guess you had to be there."

That would have been awkward.

"I think I get the picture," I say. "Your turn."

She sobers in a few seconds, and her mouth gradually flattens into a soft line.

"What's your greatest regret?" she asks softly.

"You're kidding, right?" I turn my knees in, pressing my back against the side of the cart so I can see her squarely. "I ask you a funny sex question, and you go for the jugular with this?"

"You didn't place any prerequisites on it."

"I didn't know I was dealing with a sadist, or I would have."

"Well, you didn't." She smiles a little, her eyes softening. "Greatest regret, and you have to be honest. Not something stupid like never seeing *The Goonies*."

"God, of course I've seen *The Goonies*." I run a hand over my face, scouring all the regrets crowding my past to find the one that's the worst. And once I have it, I'm not sure I want to be honest with her. If I am, it means I have to be honest with myself, too.

"Okay." I cross my arms over my chest, tipping my head back to contemplate the stars in the darkening sky. "I was like, twelve years old."

"Is this gonna count?" She drops a skeptical look on me. "That's pretty young for regrets."

"Not where I come from," I say softly. I unfocus my eyes, looking back through the years until I find that day on the playground. "This cop stopped me and my cousin Jade."

"For what?"

"For . . .nothing." I shrug. "It isn't like what you're used to. They didn't need a reason. And this was in the nineties, so drugs were huge in our neighborhood. And kids our age were slinging on the playgrounds. So, we didn't think anything of it."

"What happened?"

"He searched me, and of course, found nothing. I was a good kid." A staccato laugh comes quick and short. "I watched movies, went to school, and wrote poetry. Not exactly a gangbanger in the making. My mom made sure I kept my head down and kept moving. You didn't have to find trouble in my neighborhood. It found you."

I glance over my shoulder at the ground, which is so far away the people below like a colony of ants, and turn back.

"Then the same cop searches my cousin." I pause and swallow the heat blistering my throat. "He . . .she had on this dress, and he . . .touched her."

I'll never forget Jade's indrawn breath. He'd told me to stay against the wall, to face the wall, but when I heard her gasp, I looked at them. I wasn't a rule breaker, but I knew this one time, I should break the rule. I should step in when I saw his hand working under her dress, when I saw one tear slide down her face. He had a gun. He was a cop. I didn't know what to do. Jade just shook her head at me, thinking the same thoughts and holding the same fears. It was only a few moments, but that was all it took to turn the whole world upside down.

"I don't know why we never talked about it," I say to Bristol. "And we never told anyone. Jade didn't want to. She was ashamed, I think. I know I was."

"You were kids and he was in authority." There's a world of emotion in Bristol's eyes when they bore into mine. "That's awful."

I blink away the tears filling my eyes as that day suffocates me again.

"And some days, I look in the mirror, like just brushing my teeth or whatever, and I'll say it out loud. I'll say 'Don't touch her.' Just like that. Just that, and maybe he would have stopped."

But there's no rewind button. There are no do-overs. There's no delete key that undoes the damage or the guilt or the shame. I'm sorry, but I can't make it un-happen, and that's why it's called regret.

"Things just kind of changed after that, between me and Jade, I mean," I say. "I mean, we still talk, but . . ."

I shrug, giving up on words to articulate my complex relationship with the cousin I still love so much.

"We all make mistakes and do things we wish we could do differently," Bristol says softly, drawing my attention to her pretty face in the carnival light. "That's part of life. You and Jade should talk about it someday. Tell her you're sorry it happened, and that given the chance, you would have done things differently. We only get one life, but it's filled with second chances. That's why I came here to try again with Rhyson."

I don't reply, but we smile, and I want to tell her that I've never spoken about this before. I want to tell her how good it felt and that I could talk to her all day. That this wheel could be stuck up in the sky for hours, and I wouldn't get tired of hearing her talk or watching her listen.

I look over the side of the car again, wishing I could hurl this shame and hurt down to the ground but knowing I'll live with it forever. Even though it has faded through the years, it isn't gone. It won't ever go away completely, but at least today, for the first time, I shared this load.

And it feels lighter.

12

BRISTOL

I SHOULDN'T HAVE ASKED that question. "I'm sorry."

I whisper it, but Grip hears. He's looking over the side, maybe composing himself. There were tears in his eyes when he talked about his cousin Jade, and that dark, dirty day. When he looks back to me, his eyes are clear of tears but they are still shaded with emotion.

"Sorry for what?"

"For asking you ..." I lift one shoulder, hoping it conveys things I can't put into words. "I'm nosy. It gets me in trouble. I ask too many questions, and then I—"

"I like it," he cuts in softly.

My breath swirls around in my chest and furiously circles my heart like a cyclone.

"You ...you like what?" I ask.

"That you're curious and ask questions that make me think. That challenge me. People don't always do that."

There's a disparaging twist to my lips. "Because it's called casual conversation," I say with a husky laugh. "And I seem to have trouble keeping things casual."

With you.

I don't say the words aloud, but our eyes exchange them none-theless.

"It just means I get to ask a tough question that will gut you." He delivers the words lightly, but the curiosity in his eyes is real. This will be a gutter.

"Okay." I release a long-suffering sigh. "I guess it's only fair. Hit me with your best shot."

"Toughest day of your life." He twists so his back is against the car and he has a clear view of me.

"Wow. Just go for it, huh?"

"Like you didn't?" He cocks one brow and props his chin in his hand, as if he has all the time in the world to wait.

"Right." I laugh nervously. "This is the last question. No more after this."

"And I was honest with you, so repay the favor." He says it easily, but the remnants of emotion on his face remind me it's true.

"Toughest day of my life." I twist a little to face him, too, which is probably good because, if I look over the side, I might start hyperven-tilating again. "Um, the day Rhyson left."

It's quiet for a moment, and I give him my face to search, not looking down or away. So he'll know it's true.

"Grady had been visiting us for the holidays." I look down at the anxious tangle of my fingers on the safety bar. "And he took Rhyson with him when he left."

Rhyson wasn't home much, but when he was, I could always find him in one of two places: his rehearsal room or the tree house in our back-yard. I ran from room to room. I climbed that tree looking for him, but he was nowhere to be found, and no one had even bothered to tell me.

"What I remember most is the silence." I hush my voice like it's a secret, and maybe it is, because I've never told anyone this before. "Rhyson rehearsed constantly when he was home."

I laugh, but it costs me a pain in my chest right above my heart.

"I was such a goofball I would sit out in the hall and listen to him play for hours while I did my homework, painted my nails, or even talked on the phone with my friends."

I rest my elbows on the safety bar and prop my chin on the heel of my hand.

"That was when I felt closest to him. I know that sounds crazy since we weren't even in the same room when he was playing, but his music was the realest thing about him. And not in a concert hall or in front of an audience. It was most honest, most raw, when he was alone. It was just for him."

A sigh trembles across my lips and is absorbed by the cooling night air.

"And I would pretend it was just for me, too. So when Grady took him away . . ." I hear my mother's influence, her anger even in how I phrase that, so I amend. "When Rhyson left, the house was dead. No music, no life. He left without even saying goodbye."

Hot tears leak from the corners of my eyes.

"To me, I mean." My breath stutters as I struggle to get the words out. "I am his twin, Grip. Somehow I, this unremarkable in every way girl who couldn't even play a clarinet 'adequately', shared a womb, shared the beginning of my life with this genius person, and I feel it so deeply. It's like I feel his music, I feel him the way twins feel each other."

I bite my bottom lip to control its trembling. "But he doesn't feel me."

"He does, Bristol." Grip reaches over to grab my hands, his one hand, which is so much bigger, darker, and rougher than mine, is a comfort. "I know he loves you. He's just ... like you said, a genius. Musicians, sometimes the art takes so much from us and we don't know how to save enough for the people around us. We pour so much into it, it's isolating, especially for Rhyson. He was a kid. Dealing with more shit than most adults ever have to. The kind of pressure that had him popping pills just to survive it."

I know truth when I hear it, and what Grip says is true. I just stare back at him, giving him permission to go on.

"Rhyson's addiction was a destructive path, and your parents weren't helping. They may not have realized it, but they were only making it worse." Grip dips his head to catch my eyes as he says the next part. "You said Grady took him, but he saved Rhyson. You know that, right?"

I do know that. For the first time, I allow the worst-case scenario to play out in my head. If Rhyson hadn't left, hadn't gone to rehab, or hadn't gotten the help he needed, what would have happened? God, I've made this all about me. All about how I felt when Rhyson left, not how desperate he must have been to go. All these years, I thought my heart was broken, but only for myself. For the first time, maybe ever, my heart breaks for the gifted, lonely boy who had nothing but his piano.

I mop my hands over my cheeks, gathering the wetness on my palms. So many tears. I've never told anyone how I felt that day. My mother tried to make me go to therapy for that, too, but by then I was sixteen with a strong will of my own and refused. I was tired of talking to strangers, and I wanted to keep this pain locked away, private.

Until now. Until Grip. His eyes rest on my face. I feel his compassion, and it weighs so much I want out from under it. I turn my head to escape the honesty between us for a few seconds. Just for a reprieve. As soon as I look over the side, I realize my mistake.

"Oh, God. We're so high."

Breath charges up my throat, panic pushing out the last few minutes of peace. My heart jackhammers. Blood rushes to my head, and the world spins. I grip my head to make it stop.

"Hey, hey." Grip scoots closer, eliminating the distance between us. "Put your head down as far as you can."

The safety bar keeps me from putting my head between my knees, but I don't think it would help anyway. Nothing helps. It's irrational. I know I'm safe, but fear mocks me and makes me its bitch. I hate it, but I can't stop it.

"My mom used to tell me to recite things," Grip says from above me. "Like to distract myself when I was scared. To give me something else to focus on."

It only makes me more anxious that I have nothing I can recite. Fear jumbles all my thoughts together, so discombobulated that I can't even assemble the digits of my phone number.

"I can't think of anything."

"Okay. Hold up." He rubs my back in soothing strokes that don't soothe. "I'll do it. Just listen to my voice. Focus on what I'm saying."

I can't focus. I can't stop the encroaching darkness, blurring my edges and knotting my interior. It's never been this bad, and it would happen right in front of Grip.

"I'll recite 'Poetry' by Pablo Neruda. My favorite, actually." Grip's voice is warm but disembodied as I press my eyes closed. "It feels like he was writing my life story. Like he knew there would be this kid who needed something bigger than himself, and he wrote this to guide that kid to a different path. This has always felt like more than a poem. It's personal. It feels like my prophecy."

The emotion, the honesty in his voice compels me to hazard a glance at him. In the faint light of the moon and the bright lights of the carnival, I see his face. Beautiful and bronzed, a sculpture of bold bones and full lips. His eyes are intent, never looking away from mine as he begins.

His deep voice caresses Neruda's sentiments of how poetry called him from the street and away from violence. Of how writing saved him from a certain fate and opened up a world he'd never imagined. And Grip's right. The poem could have been written for him ... could have foretold the story of a boy called, not from the streets of a Chilean city, but from the streets of Compton.

Passion weaves between his words and conviction laces every line. He means these words. He loves these words. Amazingly, as he's reciting a poem I've never heard before, someone else's words illuminate Grip to me. I see him clearly. A man deeply committed to his craft and who views his gift as a miracle of circumstance. As cocky as he is, I see him humbled by the means to escape a path so many others never leave. And if the poem tells his story, his eyes are a confession, never straying from mine, holding mine in the moonlight, his voice liquid poured over something sweet. As he approaches the end, my fears are forgotten, but I'm still stuck on a Ferris wheel under a darkened sky, and nothing has ever been more fitting than the final words, in which the poet says he wheeled with the stars and his heart broke loose on the wind.

There are too few perfect moments in this life. Far too few of us get them, but I am privileged to have this one with this man. When he empties his chest of his heart and empties his body of his soul for me under a starry sky on a Ferris wheel. And I know. In this moment, I know that I'm lost to him. It has been a matter of days. It has been a string of moments. It has not been long enough to tell him, but in my heart, I know I am lost.

"Did that help?" he asks.

He searches through the dim light for my fear or my panic, but they aren't there anymore. He leans closer, so close his breath whispers over my face. I don't know when he realizes that fear has gone and that something else has come, but I see the change in his eyes.

I think he might be lost in me, too.

The inches between our lips disappear. At the first brush of his mouth on mine, I know this kiss will never end. It will live on in my memory for the rest of my life. His lips beg entry, a tentative touch that blazes through my defenses and hastens the rhythm of my heart. I clutch his arm, skin and muscle, satin over steel. A thousand textures collide. The hot silk of his mouth. The sharp, straight edge of his teeth. The firm curve of his lips. The taste of him. God, the taste of him makes me moan. He cups my face, fingers spearing into my hair. I press so close the heat of his body burns through the thin fabric of our shirts.

"Bris." He says it against my lips before trailing kisses down my chin. His mouth opens over my neck, hot and wet, and I arch into him, the pleasure like a train in my veins. Rushing. Vaulting. Exploding.

"Oh, God." I'm a panting mess. My hands venture under his shirt, desperate, nails scraping at his back. "Keep kissing me."

He's back at my lips, devouring, our tongues dueling, dancing. This kiss has a cadence, his head moving to the left and then right, on beat, a syncopation, a simultaneity of lips and tongues. His mouth slants over mine, hot and zealous, and I link my fingers behind his head, clinging, afraid this will end. Afraid to lose the enormity of this moment. At the top of the world, so close we could almost touch the sky and with only the stars watching, I found out what a kiss should be.

13

GRIP

I'M SO SCREWED.

I kissed Bristol last night, and nothing's the same. Our kiss ended once the wheel started turning, but nothing stopped. There's a momentum to this thing between Bristol and me that I can't stop. I don't want to stop. We held hands through the Ferris wheel's slow, rolling descent to the ground. By silent agreement, we let go when we saw the others. I don't want this examined, mocked, made light, and for now, we want to keep it to ourselves.

The rest of the night, we stayed with the group, but a quiet, untraceable intimacy linked us. We played silly games and won stupid prizes. She won me a black plastic watch. I won her a whistle. We got lost together in the fun house, and I pressed her against a wavy mirror. Even distorted, our shapes were perfect together.

I don't know what to do. I don't know what she wants or what I am to her. Is she slumming? Am I some exotic fruit or a novelty she sampled on vacation? Or does this feel to her like it feels to me? Like the beginning of something. Mr. Chocolate Charm himself can't get up the nerve to ask a girl if she really likes him.

I watch her and Jimmi running on the shore, laughing as the tide chases them. Jimmi's uncle has a small beach house in Malibu, and we're spending Bristol's last day here. Rhyson spent the day with us but got called into the studio for one more tweak. It's been a perfect day, except I've had no time with Bristol alone to ask her what she's thinking or feeling. She leaves tomorrow, and I don't know if we'll forget this ever happened, or if we'll make it something more.

"Whew." Jimmi collapses onto the beach blanket. "This day has been amazing."

"It's gorgeous here," Bristol smiles and sits beside Jimmi. "Thank you for bringing me."

Our eyes collide over the small fire we used to roast marshmallows and s'mores. She looks quickly away and lies down to close her eyes.

"We need to be heading back," Luke says, his arm around Mandi's shoulders. "One last swim before we go? Not too far out because it's already dark."

"Let's make it count," Jimmi says, a reckless glint in her eye. "Skinny-dipping."

Luke and I are already shaking our heads. No way am I going bare nuts into that freezing water.

"I'm not going naked into the ocean," Mandi says. "There's seaweed and fish and it's cold. No, thanks."

"What about you?" Jimmi nudges Bristol, who still lies back, eyes closed. "You chicken?"

"Those mind games don't work on me." Bristol sits up, a defiant smile curling the edges of her full lips. "Do you honestly think I'd let you goad me into such a stupid dare?"

They look at each other, exchanging wicked grins and then scrambling to their feet, a blur of long legs and flying bikini tops. My jaw unhinges. I can't believe she did that. It looks like she kept the bottom on, but I can clearly see her top, which is nothing more than two tiny triangles of fabric, on the beach with Jimmi's. Their squeals echo in the night.

"You wanna?" Mandi asks Luke, sporting a reckless grin of her own now.

For a moment, Luke looks like he'll resist, but his eyes wander to the bikini tops on the sand and then to Mandi's considerable rack.

"Hey, why not?" He shrugs, standing to his feet and shucking off his trunks. I look away, not needing to see his tan line or his junk. I deliberately avert my eyes when Mandi tosses her top and runs to the ocean's edge.

I look to the shore, making out their bodies, shadows in the fresh moonlight, frolicking and screaming and laughing. A smile settles on my lips, and I'm on my feet walking toward the water. Not naked, though. It's too cold for that shit.

I've waded in just a few feet, still adjusting to the temperature of the water, when an arm slips around my waist from behind. Warm, water-slick breasts press into my back.

"Bristol?" I ask in a voice that is husky and hopeful.

"No, it's Jimmi, you doofus." Bristol's voice is playful, her chuckle full of mischief as she slips away, deeper into the water, a little farther from shore.

We're not too far out, but I don't see or hear the others as I turn to face her. The night cloaks her. There isn't enough moonlight to see her clearly, but I sense her. I sense her craving because it matches mine. It's her last night here, and I'll be damned if she's leaving without kissing me again. I press through the water's resistance until our bodies are flush. Her nipples, tight from the cool night air, and maybe from desire, pebble against my chest. I dip my head and leave my words in her ear.

"I want to kiss you again."

Her sharp breath is her only reply, but I rest my lips against hers to taste her consent. Palming her sides, my fingers almost meeting at her back, I stretch my thumbs up to rub her nipples, alternating between strokes brisk then slow.

"Oh, God, yes." She spreads her hands over my shoulders and to my neck, urging my head down. "Kiss them. Please kiss them."

I slip my hands over her ass and lift her out of the water so she can lock her legs at my back, scooting her up until I can take one nipple into my mouth.

Shiiiiiiiit.

I open wide, taking as much of her into me as I can, sucking the nipple and licking at the silky halo of surrounding skin.

"Grip, yes." Her hands claw at my shoulders and run up my neck. She dips her head to possess my mouth with hers. Her kiss woos me in the water. Her fingers on my skin are poetry. Her lips, prose. The rhythm of her heart against mine, iambic. Every touch, eloquence.

The current tugs at our bodies as the tide comes in, and clinging to each other, we let the flow take us. With our mouths still fused, legs still tangled, tongues hungry and twisting together, we drift into deeper waters.

Complex and effortless.

My own words come back to haunt me, describing a rapper's flow. I can't help but compare it to what's passing between us in the deep. The unexpected alchemy that's been flowing between us since the moment we met. It's layered and complicated, and yet, there's no struggle, no force. It feels easy. Effortless. It feels so good, I can't imagine this ending.

"I need to know," I mumble at the underside of her breast. "What we're doing, Bristol."

"What do you mean?" she gasps. "This feels fantastic."

I slide her down my body and frame her face in my hands. "Is this like some spring break fling for you?" I ask earnestly.

"Grip, I . . ." She drops her forehead to my chest, and I would give anything to turn up the wattage on the moon so I could see her face better. So I could see her eyes. "I don't know."

It shouldn't hurt. We shared a few days, a few conversations, and the best kisses of my life. That's it. That's all, but last night feels like the best night I've ever had. And to think it wasn't monumental for her or that she's "deciding" what we'll be when I feel like the decision was made for me almost as soon as I laid eyes on her, hurts.

"I'm not a casual kind of person." She sighs, and I can imagine the jaded look on her face. "And there's a lot that could go wrong. You're my brother's best friend. I'm moving here and it could be awkward if things . . . go south."

"They won't," I assure her. "Just give it a chance."

"What?" She lets out a cynical laugh. "A long-distance relationship?"

"Why not?"

"You're a player for one thing, Mr. Bees with honey and chocolate. You get bored, you move on, and you probably cheat."

There's a question in her voice, and I know this is the moment when I should tell her about Tessa. But I'm having such a hard time even getting her to consider making us an us, and I don't want to make it any harder by throwing that wrench in the works. I'll deal with Tessa as soon as Bristol is gone.

"It'd be different with you." I run a palm over her wet hair. "I know it would be."

"But I don't know it would be, and . . ." I see the shape of her head as she lifts it, shaking it. "Can we take it slow? I don't want to get hurt, and I think you could hurt me really badly."

Her answer is soft and honest, and it only makes me want her more.

"We can do that." I bend to kiss her neck, sucking at the salt-covered skin until she gasps, grinding her hips through the water seeking me. That's her spot. One of them. She wants to take it slow? I'm willing to take my time finding all the others.

14

BRISTOL

TAP, TAP, TAP.

I look up from the suitcase I'm packing. Someone's knocking on the door of Grady's guest bedroom. I hastily tuck the cheap whistle Grip won for me at the carnival into the bag and zip it up. When I open the door, Rhyson stands in the hall.

"Can I come in?" His dark hair, always a gorgeous mess, flops into his eyes.

"Sure." I step back and wave him in, sitting on the bed and waiting to hear what he has to say. We've had very little time alone since the night we talked after the club. We spent yesterday with his friends, and he had to go back to the studio last night.

"All packed, huh?" He eyes my huge suitcase.

"Looks that way." A small, sad smile touches my mouth. "I'll miss LA. Who'd have thought?"

"Will you miss LA, or will you miss your big brother?" he teases.

"Not this big brother stuff again."

"I haven't been much of one." His smile fades. "A brother, I mean."

Instead of answering, I wait for him to go on.

He shakes his head. "It's so hard to know what to trust when it comes to them, to our parents."

"You can trust me to be who I say I am, Rhyson. Your sister." I tilt my chin and flash him some confidence in the form of a smile. "You'll see that when I'm managing that career for you."

"I don't have a career." He laughs and leans back on the bed, propped on his elbows.

"But you will. You should. And when you do, I'll be right there to help you."

"You can't build plans around something that hasn't happened yet."

"Idiot, what do you think dreams are if not plans we make based on things that haven't happened yet?"

We laugh a little, and I lie back beside him, resting my head on his shoulder. What I wouldn't have given years ago to have my brother like this. To have time with him when he wasn't rehearsing or touring or doing whatever was required of him.

"Don't you have any dreams of your own?" he asks.

Grip's face, his soft touches, and promises in the dark waters last night, come to mind. I want to believe him because those kisses on the Ferris wheel, in the fun house, in the ocean were the best of my life. The conversations we've had this week changed me. No controversy, no memory, no hope or fear was off-limits. They have woven themselves—he has woven himself—into the fabric of my dreams so quickly it frightens me.

"I do have dreams," I finally answer. "And they're all here now."

He smiles at me slowly and nods.

"We better get going." Rhyson glances at his watch, and it makes me think of the cheap watch I won for Grip last night. I shake off memories of the carnival as Rhyson rolls the Louis bag out of my room and down the hall.

"It's a shame I didn't get to see Uncle Grady this trip."

"Next time," Rhyson says. "But there are some people who want to tell you goodbye."

When we enter the living room, my new friends are all there. Jimmi, Luke, Mandi, and standing at the back of the group is Grip, his eyes a beautifully laid trap I stumble into and can't wriggle free of. "Oh, you guys." I wrap my arms around Jimmi, who squeezes me so tightly I can barely breathe.

"I feel like I found a new bestie." Jimmi blinks tears from her big blue eyes. "We have to talk every week, and you have to come back soon. And I can come to New York, too."

"Deal." I smile through a few tears of my own. "We'll stay in touch. Don't worry."

I haven't spent as much time with Luke and Mandi, but it's still sweet of them to show up to say goodbye to me. They're both cool, and Rhyson is lucky to have this tight-knit circle of people in his life. I don't really have anything like them in New York, and it makes me want to wish away the next two years at Columbia so I can move here right away.

And then there's Grip.

We take a few careful steps toward each other, and I feel like everyone's watching us.

"Thank you for everything," I say softly, leaving a few inches between us. His eyes burn a mute plea for more.

"No problem. Sure."

He glances down at the floor before slipping his arms around my waist and dragging me against his warm, hard body. Not caring what Rhyson or anyone else thinks, I tip up on my toes and hook my elbows behind his neck as tightly as I can. His hands spread over my back, fitting my curves to all his ridges and planes.

"You come back to me, okay?" he whispers in my ear. "Slow doesn't mean stop, right?"

My cheeks fire up, and I glance self-consciously at the others, but they aren't paying attention. Rhyson is rolling my suitcase out to the car, and Mandi, Luke, and Jimmi are talking about last night at the beach swimming nude. Or semi-nude. Jimmi was the only one brave/crazy enough to be fully naked.

"No, slow doesn't mean stop," I agree. "In fact—"

His phone ringing interrupts me telling him I plan to come back this summer when I have a few days off from my internship.

"Lemme grab this," he says, frowning at the phone. "It's Jade."

I remember her name from the story he told me on the Ferris wheel. The one he still feels guilt over.

"Hey, whassup?" He presses the phone to his ear, and his brows snap together. "Why'd you tell her I was here?"

I turn away, heeding Rhyson's call to come on or I'll miss my flight. We walk outside to load up the car so we can get on the road. Rhyson and Grip are taking me, and I'm not sure if we should tell Rhyson what has been going on or not. It feels like such a fledgling thing but still substantial enough that he should know. I'm still silently debating when a Toyota Camry pulls up to the curb, and a curvy woman with dark brown skin and black, curly hair gets out. A scowl mars her beautiful face, and anger has her arms swinging at her side with her long strides.

"Where is he?" she demands of Rhyson without any preamble.

"Uh, hey, Tessa." Rhyson glances up the driveway and widens his eyes meaningfully at his best friend.

Rhyson may be looking at Grip, but Grip is looking at me, and if I didn't know better, I would say he's panicking. Before I have time to process what's happening, how my world is about to be ripped into tiny pieces, Tessa begins her tirade.

"How you gonna ignore my calls and text messages?" Yelling, she fits her hands to the swell of her hips. "For two damn weeks, Grip?"

"I didn't." Grip looks at me with troubled eyes over her shoulder and then back to her face. "We just kept missing each other. What's going on? What's this about?"

"This is about me trying to tell you something I wanted to talk about in person, not over some voice mail." Her strident voice pitches across the yard at him.

"Okay, damn, Tessa," Grips says, irritation evident on his face. "I'm going with Rhyson to take his sister to the airport. Can we talk later? When I get back?"

"Who is she?" I whisper to Rhyson.

"That's Tessa." Rhyson stretches his eyebrows until they disappear under his unruly hair. "Grip's girlfriend."

"His girl—"

I choke on the rest of the word as a tight hand vises my throat. That can't be. Last night's water-dappled promises and sea salt kisses. The perfect kiss under the stars at the top of the world. All lies? We shared deep, dark lonely things. We shared everything, and it was the most honest connection I've ever had with anyone. And under it all was the lie that he could be mine? That maybe I could be his? That he didn't belong to someone else? He would have said.

"No, we can't talk when you get back," Tessa snaps. "We need to talk now. I'm sick of chasing your ass down. You are taking responsibility for this."

"Responsibility?" Grip shakes his head and shrugs "For what?"

"For this baby, that's for what," she retorts with harsh smugness.

His wide eyes snap to my face, and any doubt that she might be the one lying, that somehow this is all a prank, a hidden camera stunt, dissolve. That guard I forgot about and dropped all week falls back into place over my heart just in time.

"We don't cry in front of strangers."

My mother's admonition, the voice of reason in my head that I ignored the last few days, slips iron discs between my vertebrae.

"Rhyson, can we go?" I ask. "I can't miss my flight home." "Bristol!" Grip yells over the screeching banshee with wildly

gesticulating arms in front of him. "Wait. I can—"

I open the door to Rhyson's car and get in, not wanting to hear the dollar-late, day-short explanations disguising his lies.

Rhyson gets in, glancing over his shoulder at the spectacle on the yard, the beautiful woman screaming at Grip's rigid face and ticking jaw. He looks at me through the car window, his eyes begging me for something I won't give.

Second chances.

"Drive, Rhyson." My voice is rock and resolve. "Let your friend sort his shit out. I'm going home."

***

The journey is just beginning!

GRIP & STILL, books 2 and 3, are up next!

*You can grab all 3 Books + Bonus Material
in the BOX SET!
"Future Glimpse" Chapters only in
enhanced Box Set!
FREE IN KU*
US: https://amzn.to/2Gh3Rrs
Worldwide: http://mybook.to/TheGripBoxSet

Individual Books FREE in KU!

*FLOW (Grip #1)
GRIP (Grip #2)
STILL (Grip #3)*

**Audiobooks available for all 3 titles.
Check Audible Escape to listen FREE with subscription!*

ALSO BY KENNEDY RYAN

The SOUL Trilogy

Want Rhyson's story? Two musicians chasing their dreams and catching each other?

Dive into the Soul Trilogy!

(Rhyson + Kai)

(FREE in Kindle Unlimited)

My Soul to Keep (Soul 1)*

Down to My Soul (Soul 2)*

Refrain (Soul 3)

Available in Audible Escape!

ALL THE KING'S MEN WORLD

Love stories spanning decades, political intrigue, obsessive passion. If you loved the TV show *SCANDAL*, this series is for you!

The Kingmaker (Duet Book 1: Lennix + Maxim)

FREE in KU!

Ebook, Audio & Paperback

mybook.to/TheKingmakerKindle

The Rebel King (Duet Book 2: Lennix + Maxim)

FREE in KU!

Ebook, Audio & Paperback

mybook.to/RebelKingKindle

Queen Move (Standalone Couple: Kimba + Ezra)

https://geni.us/QueenMovePlatforms

The Killer & The Queen

(Standalone Novella - Grim + Noelani)

Coming Soon!

(co-written with Sierra Simone)

www.subscribepage.com/TKandTQ

HOOPS Series

(Interconnected Standalone Stories set in the explosive world of professional basketball!)

LONG SHOT (A HOOPS Novel)

Iris + August's Story

Ebook, Audio & Paperback:

https://kennedyryanwrites.com/long-shot/

BLOCK SHOT (A HOOPS Novel)

Banner + Jared's Story

Ebook, Audio & Paperback

http://kennedyryanwrites.com/block-shot/

HOOK SHOT (A HOOPS Novel)

Lotus + Kenan's Story

Ebook, Audio & Paperback

http://kennedyryanwrites.com/hook-shot/

HOOPS Holiday (A HOOPS Novella)

Avery + Decker's Story

http://kennedyryanwrites.com/hoops-holiday/

Order Signed Paperbacks

THE BENNETT SERIES

When You Are Mine (Bennett 1)

Loving You Always (Bennett 2)

Be Mine Forever (Bennett 3)

Until I'm Yours (Bennett 4)

ACKNOWLEDGMENTS

THERE ARE SO many people to thank this time around. There are always lots of people, but especially with this book because I needed so much. I needed perspectives, and you always had them to offer, Teri Lyn, Joanna, Lucy. Your input was invaluable in the early stages. You lived through so many iterations of this book you will probably barely recognize the final product. If there is anything good about it, though, please know you had a hand in it through your constructive honesty and patience with my writer neuroses. Margie, thank you for ALWAYS being in my corner and cheering me on and convincing me that I'm at least a halfway decent writer on days when I feel anything but. Your friendship is so precious to me. Mary Ruth, thank you for bringing so many of my words to life with your designs and all the tireless work you volunteered to do for me. For reading early and giving me wonderful feedback: Shamika, Sheena, Shelley, Michelle. Melissa and Val, thank you for helping with the Rabble Rousers, for giving direction, and making things fun when I can't even. LOL! And thank you to the Rabble Rousers and all the supportive folks in my reader group. You are my safe place. To the authors who supported me, answered my questions, read for me, told me to pull back or to press ahead, you're the bomb. Isabelle Richards, Mandi Beck,

Adriana Locke (#AddyOnTheSide), Corinne Michaels (Boo Biscuit), and Danielle Allen. To Heather of L. Woods PR for enduring my control freak-work-around-the-clock-edness. I know I'm a piece of work, and you put up with me wearing a smile ... and pink hair! LOL! Thank you, love. I could keep going, but this would become interminable, and I really want you to start reading this book! There are too many bloggers, readers, and authors who have impacted and influenced me to name. Thank you for being in my life and a part of what I do. It means the world!

ABOUT THE AUTHOR

Connect With Kennedy!

I'm in my reader group on Facebook EVERY DAY and share all the inside scoop there first.
I'd love to meet you there: bit.ly/KennedyFBGroup

Mailing List
Like On Facebook
Instagram
Twitter
Bookbub
Follow on Amazon
Book+Main
Goodreads

New Release Text Alert:
Text Kennedy Ryan to 797979

A RITA® Award Winner, *USA Today* and *Wall Street Journal* Bestselling Author, Kennedy Ryan writes for women from all walks of life, empowering them and placing them firmly at the center of each story and in charge of their own destinies. Her heroes respect, cherish and lose their minds for the women who capture their hearts. Kennedy and her writings have been featured in *Chicken Soup for the Soul, USA Today, Entertainment Weekly, Oprah Magazine, TIME* and many others. As an autism mom, she has a special passion for raising

Autism awareness. The co-founder of LIFT 4 Autism, an annual charitable book auction, she has appeared on *Headline News*, *The Montel Williams Show*, NPR and other media outlets as an advocate for ASD families.

She is a wife to her lifetime lover-husband and mother to an extraordinary son.

Made in the USA
Middletown, DE
17 November 2024